WHISPERING WILLOWS

Also by Kimila Kay

STONEYBROOK MYSTERIES

Redneck Ranch (2023)

Five Golden Rings (2023)

MÉXICO MAYHEM SERIES

Peril in Paradise (2019)

Malice in Mazatlán (2022)

Vanished in Vallarta (2023)

ANTHOLOGIES

"Happy Birthday" Harbinger (2023)

"Table Talk" Guests (2022)

"Hates Kids" A Cup of Comfort for Mothers (2010)

"Burying Bea" A Cup of Comfort, Grieving Heart (2010)

"The Apology" A Cup of Comfort, Single Mothers (2008)

Whispering Willows is Kimila Kay's latest offering in the Stoneybrook Mysteries series. Kimila has a unique way of captivating the vulnerability, as well as strength, of her characters. I also find it intriguing to watch as some characters discover things about themselves they could not have imagined would be true. Whispering Willows is a great read! *~ Mary Eastman*

STONEYBROOK MYSTERIES REVIEWS

Five Golden Rings is an intriguing holiday story, and I couldn't wait to know who killed Santa. With each book I've read, **Kimila Kay** has honed her writing skills and continues to craft engaging tales. I can't wait for her next release, whether it's set in México or in the adorable town of Stoneybrook. *~ Ruth DeHaven*

Kimila Kay's holiday mystery, **Five Golden Rings** brings us back to Stoneybrook where her entertaining characters are all wondering who killed Santa. And if the town will be able to celebrate a Merry Christmas! *~ Cindy Schmid*

Redneck Ranch is one of those books that is hard to put down. It's a murder mystery with a sense of humor and a romance to boot! The story has engaging characters, along with a farm and a small town setting that seems familiar. A must read! *~ Gina Greb*

WHISPERING WILLOWS

A Novella

STONEYBROOK MYSTERIES-BOOK THREE

KIMILA KAY

www.KimilaKay.com
author@kimilakay.com

Windtree Press
http://windtreepress.com
info@windtreepress.com

Cover Art by *James McCracken*

Whispering Willows, Stoneybrook Mysteries, Book 3

Published in the United States of America – History:
ISBN 978-1-962065-42-9
1st Release: April 1, 2024

DEDICATION

Dedicating this novella to my beloved Aunt Cindy Conner is a very small way of honoring a fabulous woman who left us too soon.

When I married Randy, thirty-three years ago, Aunt Cindy sent me a note wishing us a long and happy life together. She'd ended her missive with, "Remember to laugh, even during the difficult times, because laughter is the key to a happy marriage."

Not too long after we were married, Randy and I were arguing. He finally threw up his hands and said, "If you keep using long-ass words I have to look up in a dictionary, I'm done." Needless to say, we laughed … a lot!

But the best advice my Aunt Cindy gave to all of us, was … "Shut up and Love!"

The truth whispered through the weeping willows. An echo undiscernible to the human ear, but the truth, nonetheless. An unimaginable revelation regarding the disappearance of Willow Atwood. Just listen … listen to the whispering weeping willows.

WHISPERING WILLOWS

CHAPTER ONE

Echo stared at the screen but didn't react to the news.

Wyatt knew the young woman rarely spoke and never about the disappearance of her sister Willow. She touched the laptop screen with a finger then looked at him, tears in her light gray eyes. The monitor showed a picture of a tattered pink T-shirt featuring a brown bear holding a bouquet of daisies. It was the shirt their mom remembered Willow wearing the day she disappeared.

"Since it's Saturday, we won't know the identity of the remains for a few days." Wyatt hoped if he approached her in a calm manner Echo would be able to discuss the awful day her sister went missing. "It would help if we had your DNA for comparison." His knee bumped Echo's when he turned to look at Derrick, standing at the ready with a buccal swab.

"Open your mouth wide." Derrick stepped closer to Echo. "And I'll swab your cheek."

Echo looked at Derrick, then Wyatt. Nodding at Derrick, she parted her lips. A hint of tuna drifted on her breath.

Derrick angled the swab toward Echo, who leaned back, her eyes round and wary.

"Say ah," Derrick instructed. When she complied, he inserted the long swab and did a quick circle against her cheek, then slid the collection tool into a paper sleeve.

"I'll prepare this for the crime lab." Derrick walked to his desk.

Echo wiped her lips with the back of her hand and looked at the computer screen again.

"Do you know if Willow had any broken bones?" Wyatt asked.

"No." Echo tilted her head. "I mean, I don't remember." Tears trickled down her cheeks.

Wyatt handed her a tissue box as Derrick joined them.

"Willow fell from her bike." Derrick looked at Echo as if he expected her to agree.

"How old was she?" Wyatt reached for his notepad and a pen.

"I don't …" Echo began, then shrugged.

"It was before the trip into the woods," Derrick stated. "She would have been thir—"

Echo drew her knees to her chest and began rocking back and forth in her chair. She stared straight ahead, and Wyatt knew she didn't see what was in front of her. But what had happened to her, Willow, and their friend Leah five years ago.

Wyatt looked at Derrick and worried Echo wouldn't be the only one having a meltdown in the Sheriff's station.

"Derrick." Wyatt spoke softly. "Take your seat."

Derrick nodded and moved to his desk. Wyatt placed a hand on Echo's arm. He wasn't sure if soothing her was like helping his autistic cousin, but he didn't know what else to try.

Wyatt heard Derrick crack open his usual go-to, a Diet Coke, followed by pencil scratches on paper, and knew his cousin was writing in one of his notebooks. Wyatt sipped cold coffee and waited.

Echo continued to rock but made no sound and still stared ahead. Derrick's dad, Sheriff Austin Stone, had originally assigned Wyatt and Derrick to work the incident. Blake, Wyatt's brother also joined them on the case. Wyatt wished he didn't need to review the tragic events, but his mind had already headed back in time.

News of the missing girls had reached them when Leah's hysterical mom burst into the station.

"Sheriff Stone!" Vada Keller looked around the lobby. "My Leah and her friends are missing at Willow Lake. Lara Evans dropped the girls off, then went to see her boyfriend. When she came back for them, they weren't waiting in the parking lot. I-I'm worried."

"The Sheriff is out right now, but we can help." Blake moved a chair close to Vada. "Here, have a seat."

"No, no," She shook her head, "it's going to be dark soon …"

"Do you know where they were at the lake?" Wyatt picked up his phone and started a group text to the other deputies.

"They liked to go to the willow grove for a picnic." Vada ran a hand through her unkempt hair. "I told Leah to be sure and catch a ride back with Lara." Concern accentuated the fine lines around her eyes. "It isn't safe to be there after dark."

"We'll find them, Mrs. Keller." Blake escorted her toward the door. "We need you to go home in case the girls show up at your house."

A sobbing Vada Keller left, and the sheriff's department went to work. They searched the woods until it was too dark to see—even with flashlights. The next morning Wyatt and his men were joined by Fire Chief Marcus Brennan and a few of his firefighters.

When the setting sun painted the tips of the trees orange, Wyatt worried they would have to call it a night again without finding the girls.

"Here!" Ace, one of the firefighters, had shouted. "I found Cedar!"

The search party circled the girl, who lie unconscious, but breathing. Mac enlisted his men to stabilize Cedar on the picnic blanket and radioed the ambulance parked at the lodge.

"The EMTs are on their way," Mac told Wyatt. "We'll carry her toward them," he said as his men lifted the blanket and headed for the trail.

"Keep me posted on her condition," Wyatt called after Mac.

"Copy." Mac gave a wave and followed his crew.

"Wyatt," Derrick said behind him.

"What?" He knew from the look on Derrick's face the news wasn't good.

"I found Leah." Derrick turned and walked toward a patch of daisies.

Wyatt followed his cousin to where the young girl's body lay. She was partially clothed, and Wyatt could tell her last minutes with her killer had been awful. He wanted to cover Leah to give her some dignity, but he knew that would contaminate the scene.

Derrick was already on the phone with the coroner's office. Next, he'd request the Oregon state police and Crime Scene Unit from Salem.

"Wyatt." Deputy Simms approached, carrying a backpack. "I found this next to the picnic area." He lifted the pack. "Willow's name is printed on the inside. And …" He pointed to blood on the strap.

Wyatt was jolted out of the memory when Echo shot to her feet and ran from the station.

He started to follow her, but Derrick stopped him. "Let her go. She needs to process the possibility we've found Willow's remains. Trying to talk to her will extend her shutdown."

Wyatt nodded and watched as Cedar Atwood ran down Main Street on her way back to her small house near the Babbling Brook Café.

The only girl rescued from the willow grove, Cedar, was questioned several times as they tried to piece together what had happened. Other than saying their attacker had been a boy, her only response to anything they asked was to repeat the question.

Her speech pattern had remained the same over the years, earning her the nickname Echo.

CHAPTER TWO

Harley let Elvis have the round pen all to himself as she organized the tack along the fence line, then shoveled manure into a wheelbarrow. The ginormous quarter horse followed her around like a big black dragon, curious about everything she was doing. The ten-year-old, seventeen hand Elvis was an anomaly when it came to his size. Despite his massive build, he reminded Harley of a big teenager.

Wyatt was coming to dinner, so Harley wanted to finish her long list of Saturday chores. Then she'd have an hour to get ready for their evening. Mid-May had brought warm days with cool evenings. Tonight's weather would be perfect for barbequing the T-Bones Wyatt planned to grill. She could almost taste the summer salad she had decided to make as a side dish.

As she finished rolling the hose after watering down the round pen, Harley thought about her first year as the owner of the Redneck Ranch.

She and the ranch had survived a raging fire thanks to help from Wyatt and the residents of Stoneybrook. They had originally given her the nickname *greenhorn*, but now welcomed her into the fold. Stoneybrook had seen three young women murdered over the span of seven years, but the mystery had been solved not long after Harley arrived in Stoneybrook. And now she was no longer afraid of her ancient barn where two of the bodies had been found. After her rescue from a serial killer during Christmastime, Harley and Wyatt had grown closer, finally sharing their first "I love yous."

Now, as she finished up her chores, she marveled at how uneventful the first five months of this year had been. She loved her life in Stoneybrook. Smiling, she realized, besides her mom and younger brother Harrison, the only thing she missed about New York was her bestie, Busy, who was planning a visit next week.

Elvis whinnied from the round pen, where she'd left him while cleaning his stall. After she'd acquired the gigantic horse, Wyatt had helped her expand Elvis's stall and he now had access to a small outside area. Wyatt kept encouraging Harley to ride her new horse, but she didn't think her riding skills were honed enough to manage Elvis.

Wiping sweat from her brow, she did a slow turn to make sure she hadn't forgotten to feed someone or fill their water buckets. The minis, Scarlett and Rhett, were munching hay, and Hoss, her old hog, snuffled the ground looking for scraps he'd knocked out of his dish. Pigmy goat siblings Butch and Sundance, had darted outside and found a sunny patch of grass to munch.

Her other equine charges, Maverick and Trigger, tugged hay from their feed bags, both stepping to their gates for a drive-by pet as she walked toward the round pen.

"Okay, big guy," she took Elvis by the halter, "your suite is all clean and dinner has been served."

Harley heard Buckeye and the other chickens squawking, which meant Trampas was playing his nightly game of chase. She tucked Elvis into his stall and smiled when he sniffed the fresh pine shavings. Harley held her hand up and waited for him to say goodnight. The monster horse centered the star on his forehead against her palm.

"Goodnight, Elvis." Harley removed his halter and rubbed his face until he stepped away, heading for his feed bag.

She turned off the big overhead lights, then flicked the switch for the dimmer bulbs and exited the barn. As she made her way to the stairs leading to the wraparound porch of her old farmhouse, Harley smiled at Miss Kitty and Festus, both enjoying the large cat condo she'd set up for them.

After stepping into the mudroom, she shucked her boots and grabbed a bottle of water from the fridge, then headed upstairs for a much-needed shower. First, she double-checked her outfit for the evening. Her aqua sundress paired perfectly with the new turquoise dragonfly necklace, a gift from Wyatt for her one-year anniversary at the Redneck Ranch.

Her phone chimed before she stepped into the shower, and she smiled at Busy's text.

Busy: *Changed flight to arrive tomorrow. Land Eugene at three. I'll take Uber.*

Good thing Elizabeth Benton came from money, because an Uber ride to Stoneybrook would cost her a bundle.

CHAPTER THREE

You didn't bury the bones deep enough!" his mother yelled at him.

"It was three years ago." He gave her a blank stare.

"Well, I'm guessin' with all the new-fangled DNA tests they might figure out who she is and what you did to her before—"

Her words trailed off when he came to his feet.

"I told you we shouldn't have come back here to the gulch. No telling what evidence we've left in the damn woods."

A young woman, trailed by a small child, entered the kitchen and her smile faded when he looked at her.

"I … I thought I'd start dinner."

He stepped toward her and kissed her, ignoring her recoil. The little girl grinned at him, but he didn't acknowledge her except to say, "She's filthy, give her a bath."

The young woman tucked the child behind her and muttered, "After dinner."

He headed for the door, but the old woman's nagging brought him to a halt.

"You cain't bring another girl here, not after she let the last one escape." She glared at the young woman. "It's your job to watch the girls, you dumb bitch." She yelled, spittle flying through the air.

Suppressing a smile when the young woman squared off against his mother, he barked, "Leave her alone."

She whipped around, her hand held high and ready to slap him. "Don't talk to your mother that way."

He grabbed her wrist before she could strike him, the stale odor of cigarette smoke and cheap whiskey emanating from her.

The young woman stepped back, shielding the child.

"I'll talk to you any way I want, *mother*," he growled.

He grabbed a generic beer from the fridge. Glancing at the young woman before he stalked from the rundown hovel, he said, "Come get me when my dinner is ready."

He banged through the screen door and headed for the shed he'd converted into a holding room. A tinge of anger spiked his heart rate when he thought about arriving at their previous dwelling and finding everything burned to the ground. Luckily for him, the gullies and ravines were filled with deserted buildings. This rundown collection had the perfect sized shed and a bigger shack with a kitchen. Someone had also dug a well which was a bonus. He'd been lucky to find a used 10,000-watt generator, so they had plenty of power for the ramshackle house.

Still, he thought they would've been better off staying in northern California. They hadn't yet left any bodies in the Shasta National Forest, and they had managed to move from one small town to another without drawing any attention.

His anger peaked when he thought about his mother. She was actually to blame for the girl's death. Before he could touch the girl, his mother had backhanded the kid when she wouldn't eat leftover meatloaf. The girl had fallen from her chair and hit her head on the edge of the cabinets. She wouldn't stop crying, so his mother insisted he put her in the shed. He found the young captive dead the next morning. Of course, he knew ultimately if he hadn't kidnapped her, his mother couldn't have delivered the blow that killed the young girl. And now the remains had been found.

God, how he hated his mother. All she'd ever done was make him feel inadequate. When puberty hit, she'd made him feel like a pervert for kissing a local girl. He'd tried to explain it wasn't his idea to hide in the garden shed in the girl's backyard. That he hadn't forced her to take off her clothes. Or asked her to touch him. It didn't matter what he told his mother. She'd beat him within an inch of his life, then packed up their miserable belongings and left town.

Desire, colored with shame, washed over him when he thought about the day he'd found the three girls in the willow grove. He hadn't meant to kill the first girl, but she wouldn't quit screaming. One of the friends sat crying and rocking back and forth. When he'd approached her; she jumped to her feet and ran. As he chased her down, the third friend rushed him with a big stick in her hand. The three of them had gone down in a heap and the crying girl hit her head, falling silent.

The friend with the stick struck him across the back and they fought until he gained control of her weapon. For the first time since he'd been taking advantage of young girls, he felt something other than rage. He felt respect and he knew he needed to keep the wild girl for himself.

His mother's recent berating had created a longing for someone new to enjoy, even though the last time had ended with the young woman freeing his newest captive. But he couldn't subdue the longing to take another girl.

As he sipped his beer, he thought about the young woman, a burning in his groin indicating he still enjoyed discovering new things about her. She was older now and even more beautiful than when he'd captured her. And despite fighting him every time he took her, they'd found a kind of balance. Not even the arrival of the child had deterred his desire for the girl he'd snatched from the woods five years ago.

But the evil animal living inside of him wanted a new challenge to feed his compulsion.

CHAPTER FOUR

After leaving his office for the day, Wyatt couldn't shake the image of Cedar Atwood bolting from the Sheriff's Station. And though Derrick had made it clear Wyatt shouldn't follow Echo, he worried about her. She had no one to talk to about the recently-discovered bones that might belong to her missing older sister, Willow.

Unlike the Kellers who'd moved away after their daughter Leah's murder, the Atwoods had stayed in Stoneybrook. Her parents waited for Echo to graduate high school, then decided to move to Nevada. Despite their best efforts, and with no explanation, their youngest daughter refused to make the move. Wyatt assumed Echo couldn't leave Stoneybrook until she knew what had happened to Willow.

Before Wyatt left, he asked Derrick again if he knew whether Willow had broken any bones. Although Derrick remembered her bike accident, he didn't recall her being injured, which meant she probably wasn't seen by a doctor. Wyatt would have to wait for the remains to be examined to find out about any abnormalities or damage prior to the individual's death.

As he made the turn onto the highway, he thought again about the young couple who had discovered the bones while on a hike near Willow Lake. He knew Marie Davis had moved back to Stoneybrook eight months ago with her boyfriend. The couple had bought the bait and tackle shop on the highway leading to the lake. Even though the lake's resort had been shut down, there were plenty of rivers and tributaries perfect for trout fishing, so the small shop did a steady business. He made a mental note to ask Derrick if he knew the route the couple had taken on their hike.

Making the turn onto Little Creek Road, his mind jumped to the situation that had introduced him to the beautiful owner of the Redneck Ranch. Their initial encounter had occurred thanks to her errant donkey, Maverick, escaping his stall and heading for Wyatt's ranch. Then Harley's ex-fiancé found a young woman's body on the floor of her old barn. Wyatt and his deputies conducted an investigation which led them to Carl Yates, the serial killer who had terrorized Stoneybrook for seven years. Wyatt was glad the demented murderer had met his demise at the hand of his last victim, Sylvie Owen.

He pulled into Harley's driveway and parked in front of the ancient barn. The old girl looked more inviting after the facelift his high school friend, Britt Hanson, had given the barn. Lifting the butcher bag and wine carrier from Fenya's shop, he climbed out of his truck. He was glad Ms. Petrova, who'd been instrumental in helping locate the man who'd murdered Stoneybrook's resident Santa last Christmas, had made the move to town. As he did with all the local businesses, Wyatt tried to support her store as much as possible.

The afternoon air was still warm, but he could tell the night would bring cooler temperatures. *Perfect for a fire.* He climbed the stairs to the wraparound porch and used the toe of his boot to open the screen door.

"Hi." Harley greeted him with a kiss, taking the sack with their steaks.

"Hi." Wyatt hung his hat on the rack, then followed her from the mudroom. He wondered again why he'd been blessed to have this beguiling woman in his life.

He placed the wine bag onto the kitchen counter and pulled her close for a proper hello. As he kissed her, she twined her arms around his neck and leaned into him, causing him to question whether dinner was necessary.

Harley palmed his chest and smiled at him. "Do you want a beer or a glass of wine?"

He pointed to her glass sitting next to the sink. "Beer."

"It's the new blonde ale, Sunrise Surfer, from Pelican Brewery." She padded to the fridge and pulled out a cold one. "I love that it tastes like summer."

"I love how pretty you look." He took the beer in one hand and twirled her with the other. Her sundress billowed around her legs and the fresh scent of jasmine wafted over him.

Giggling, she took a breath, then said, "Why thank you, Sheriff Stone." She opened a cupboard. "Want a glass?"

"No, thanks." He popped the top and took a long drink. "Want to sit outside for a bit before we start the steaks?"

"Yes." Harley bussed his lips, picked up her glass, and led the way through the dining room to the front porch. "How was your day?" She sat in a white wicker chair.

Sitting in a matching chair, Wyatt took a drink. He stared east across fields, now green after a fire had destroyed the vegetation a year ago.

Harley placed a hand on his thigh but didn't press him for a response. She understood his job and had, unfortunately, been personally exposed to the dreadful nature of humankind.

"I made a green salad to go with our steaks." She smiled at him. "And I have adult root beer floats planned for dessert."

Wyatt pulled her onto his lap, so she sat straddling his legs, facing him. "Sounds like the perfect dessert to be enjoyed naked in your new pool."

Harley kissed him, then said, "I'm not sure the water's warm enough."

He caressed her ass. "Naked by the fire then."

She tilted her head. "What if someone drops by?"

"Ms. Harper." He pulled her hips toward him. "Are you trying to avoid being naked with me?"

"No." Harley laughed, and he felt the vibration of her body deep in his loins. "Maybe naked before dessert would help us work up an appetite for a sweet treat." She kissed him and pressed against his crotch.

"If you kiss me like that again, I'm going to need to work up an appetite before dinner."

Harley stood and took his hand, opening the screen door that led into the foyer.

His phone buzzed. Wyatt said a silent expletive, then pulled it from his shirt pocket and looked at Derrick's text.

Derrick: *Tracked down Willow's MRs. Nurse owed me a favor. No broken bones*

Wyatt: *Copy. At Harley's if you need anything*

Derrick: *Copy*

Wyatt wondered what Derrick could've done to garner a favor from the nurse who gave him Willow's medical records. He stepped into the foyer, navigated the dining room, and found Harley in the kitchen.

"Do you have to go?" she asked as she rinsed her beer glass.

"No." Stepping close to her and wrapping his arms around her waist, he waited until she turned to him, then kissed her.

When he released her lips, he said, "Are you starving?"

Harley wrapped her arms around his waist. "Yes, but not for dinner." She kissed him, then headed for the back door. "Lock the front door before you come up."

Wyatt grinned, walked back to the foyer, and thumbed the lock. They'd learned the hard way that well-meaning visitors didn't always knock and wait for an invitation.

He took the stairs two at a time to the landing, where Harley waited for him. They held hands and climbed upstairs to her bedroom.

"I missed you." Wyatt drew her into his arms and kissed her.

"I missed you, too." Harley twined her hands in his hair and brought his lips back to hers.

He slid the strap of her sundress off her shoulder, and she pulled at his polo. He let her tug his shirt over his head. When her sundress drifted to the floor, Wyatt sucked in a breath at the site before him. She reached for the buttons on his jeans, and he kicked off his boots. Harley slid his pants off his hips and pulled him onto the bed next to her.

Wyatt nuzzled her neck and Harley moaned, holding him to her. She reached for him, and he leaned into her caress. His desire for her was evident and she grinned when she pushed him onto his back, then straddled his hips. He thought he'd explode when her softness covered him. He placed his hands on her waist and Harley set an erotic pace. Wyatt focused on waiting until she found her pleasure first. When she cried out, he brought her lips to his and found his own joy.

Harley lay snuggled under his arm, her breath warm on his chest.

"How is it that each time with you" he stroked her hair, "feels like the first time?"

"Like when we first met," she looked up at him, "and thought we should go slow, but couldn't keep our hands off of each other."

"Exactly like that." Wyatt laughed. "I'm glad we didn't go slow."

"Me too," Harley slid her hand down his torso, "because I think the anticipation of *this* might have been too much." She raised up, found his lips, and covered him with her hand.

Wyatt rolled her onto her back and moved on top of her. He kissed her as he lowered himself to meet her arching hips. They found an easy rhythm and when he looked into her eyes, Wyatt smiled at the love he saw in their amber depths.

"I love you, Ms. Harper." His words blended with her cries of ecstasy.

CHAPTER FIVE

Waking in Wyatt's arms, Harley found him smiling at her. She blinked against the bright sunshine peeking through her bedroom curtains and kissed his bare chest.

"Morning," he said, his voice still husky with sleep.

"Morning." She raised up to kiss him.

"Waking with you in my arms is the best part of my day." Wyatt stroked her back until he reached her ass.

"Same." Harley stretched out on top of him.

"As much as I would like to have a repeat of last night's appetizers for breakfast." He kissed her. "I have to go."

Brushing sandy-colored bangs from his forehead, she touched her lips to his again. "Got somewhere better to be than here?"

"Nowhere is better than here." Wyatt rolled her onto her back and caressed a breast.

His phone buzzed and she groaned. "Someone has terrible timing."

Wyatt grabbed his phone from the nightstand. He looked at the text, then kissed her before climbing from the bed.

"It's Derrick," he said, and Harley could tell by the frown creasing his brow that, though he'd rather stay with her, something pressing needed his attention.

As Harley stood, Wyatt pulled on his jeans and reached for his shirt. She plucked the shorty pajamas she normally wore to bed from a yellow overstuffed armchair, then slipped them on.

"I'll make coffee." She lifted her phone from the nightstand, kissed him, and plodded down stairs. She was a little annoyed that her romantic breakfast had been interrupted, but she'd learned over the past year that Deputy Derrick Stone never bothered his cousin if it wasn't important.

The coffee maker finished brewing a full pot of hazelnut roast as Wyatt stepped into the kitchen. His sandy-blond hair wet from a shower, he looked handsome in a clean Stone County Sheriff's polo. Knowing the departure routine of her handsome sheriff, Harley poured coffee into a travel mug.

"Thanks." Wyatt took the mug from her. "Dinner?"

"Busy's coming today instead of next week. She lands in Eugene at three, so I'll have to plan around her arrival."

"Let me guess." Wyatt tilted his head. "She's taking an Uber from the airport."

"Yes." Harley laughed. "Can you imagine the cost?"

"Yes, which means Busy can afford to buy the three of us dinner." Wyatt grinned at her.

"Where are you off to?"

"The owners of the bait and tackle shop that discovered the bones want to meet with me. Of course, *me* means *us* in

Derrick's world. They have more details to share about their discovery."

"Bones?" Harley inadvertently resorted to her hands on hips stance.

"Right." Wyatt met her questioning gaze. "I never answered your question last night about my day yesterday."

"It's okay." She held up a hand. "You don't have to share your work with me."

Wyatt stepped close to her and set the travel mug onto the counter. "Remember when we stayed at the lodge last year?"

Harley nodded, the memory of the young girl wandering in the dark along the edge of Willow Lake popping into her mind.

"The shop owners found bones near the willow grove and we're trying to determine if they belong to Willow Atwood."

"The girl who went missing over five years ago?"

"Yes." Wyatt put his hands on her arms. "I need to hear what else they have to tell us."

"Go, do your job, Sheriff," Harley bussed his lips, "because I know Echo and her parents need answers."

Wyatt wrapped her in his arms and kissed her as if he wished he could stay. "I'll text you this afternoon. Maybe we can have dinner at Rocky River to welcome Busy back to Stoneybrook."

"Good plan." Harley smiled at him.

Travel mug in hand, Wyatt headed from the kitchen. "Love you," he called as he banged through the screen door.

Harley repeated his sentiment. Since he was already on his phone, she assumed he didn't hear her. Watching through the kitchen window as he climbed into his pickup, she thought to herself, *You're a lucky girl, Harley Harper.*

After he drove away, she popped an English muffin into the toaster, poured herself a cup of coffee, then sat at the drop-leaf table. Her phone was text free for the moment. She imagined Busy hurrying through the routine of getting to her gate before texting to say she'd made her flight. On more than one occasion, Busy had been known to miss boarding by ten minutes since she had a slight time management problem.

The toaster lifted the browned muffin. Harley spread peanut butter across the top, then headed for the barn. She could hear Maverick whinnying from his stall and was thankful she wouldn't have to spend the day looking for the mischievous donkey. Of course, it helped that Wyatt's foreman, Luke Sloan, had reinforced the latch on Maverick's stall door. And another of Wyatt's ranch hands had strung hotwire along the fence line between her ranch and Broken River.

Harley inhaled the musky animal scent of the barn and greeted each member of her menagerie with a 'good morning' as she tended to them. She was glad she'd taken the extra time yesterday to clean stalls and tidy the barn. Being proactive had made today's chores go quicker.

As she headed back to the house, she plucked the rubber ducky thermometer from the pool. The water temperature was sixty-eight degrees.

"Busy will be disappointed if she can't swim in her pool," Harley told the duck before placing the yellow thermometer back into the water. The pH level was within the normal range, so all she needed was hot sunshine to warm the day and heat the pool.

Busy had insisted on paying for the installation of the above ground pool. Her bestie hoped to move to Stoneybrook at some point but wanted a pool to enjoy during her summer visits.

Crossing the patio, she checked the furniture she'd cleaned a couple of days ago. If the night provided an opportunity to swim, they could enjoy nightcaps by the fire afterward. The idea of drinks caused her thoughts to jump to jalapeño margaritas, and she ran through a mental list of ingredients.

"Oranges," Harley said as she climbed the back porch steps. She'd need to make a stop at DairyMart for oranges before she picked up Busy's champagne order from Claire at the Rocky River Bar.

She poured another cup of coffee and trekked upstairs to take a shower. Grabbing a fresh towel from the linen closet, Harley stepped into the bathroom and turned on the water. As she stood under the hot spray, the spicy scent of the body wash she'd given Wyatt for their first anniversary enveloped her.

Gooseflesh bloomed on her skin as she thought about the previous night's pre-dinner interlude. What was it about the handsome sheriff that made her feel like they were the only two people who'd ever been in love? Several obvious reasons sprang to mind, but their shared chemistry seemed otherworldly, like something no one else had ever experienced.

Despite her struggle to understand her love for him, Harley knew Wyatt Stone had been the missing puzzle piece she needed to complete her life.

CHAPTER SIX

The early Sunday morning air carried the scent of wildflowers and freshly cut grass. He was surprised the campground was almost empty, given the warm spring weather. Maybe families were waiting for the upcoming Memorial Day weekend to go camping. It was also a dry camp located along one of the many tributaries feeding Willow Lake and not everyone was cut out for boondocking.

Roaming through the vacant sites, he loaded abandoned campfire wood into his wheelbarrow. A few people were milling about. Most of them ignored him, but a few said, "Good morning."

Over the years he'd learned to wear non-descript clothing: a plain baseball cap, and work boots with a well-worn sole. He always picked rundown campgrounds that weren't well-maintained or ones that didn't have a caretaker. This allowed him to assume the role of a maintenance worker.

When he'd left the crappy shack this morning, his mother was cooking bacon and eggs. She'd yelled at him he'd better pick a girl he could control. Ignoring her warning, he snitched a piece of greasy bacon, laughing at her attempt to swat him with a spatula.

He wondered what his life would be like if he left with the young woman and the little girl. If he abandoned the bitch who'd ruined his future and left her fending for herself. He didn't have any delusions life would be full of sunshine and roses, but maybe he wouldn't be a monster who kidnapped young girls.

Or maybe he might have been able to have a normal relationship if his mother hadn't branded him a disgusting, twisted pervert. If they hadn't roamed from one rundown hovel to another. If she hadn't killed his father and made him help cover up her crime.

He'd been so busy wandering down his shitty memory lane, he'd almost missed the girl picking wildflowers in a small clearing. Sunlight sparked the red highlights in her strawberry-blonde hair. For a moment he was reminded of the young woman he'd snatched from the willow grove all those years ago.

He wanted this girl. Needed this girl. Knew the young woman would be furious with him when he brought this young girl back to the shack she'd tried to make into a home.

CHAPTER SEVEN

Wyatt and Derrick arrived at Hook, Line & Sinker and found one of the owners, Marie Davis, watering daisies in a flower box next to the door of the bait and tackle shop.

"Morning," she said, turning off the faucet.

"Ms. Davis," Wyatt extended his hand, "I believe you know Deputy Stone."

"Yes." Marie brushed a strand of honey-colored hair from her eyes and shook their hands. "Come in. I think Nate's tying flies at his worktable."

When they stepped inside, the aroma of strong coffee and a hint of anise drifted through the store. Derrick spied a table with chocolate chip cookies, and took one. They followed Marie through the tidy store to a small room in the back. Nate Long leaned over a magnifying glass as he worked on a bright pink fly.

"Nate," Marie said. "The Sheriff and Deputy Stone are here."

A tall, lanky young man, Nate set his work down and stood. "Thanks for coming."

"Derrick said you had some additional information about the bones you found."

Nate looked at his girlfriend.

"Tell him, Babe."

"It's more about the clothing scraps." Nate picked up a beautiful blue hand-tied fly. "When I was tightening the line on this fly, I remembered being struck by extra stitching on the shirt we found." He ran a finger down Marie's pink paisley tank. "Along the side seams."

"Like maybe someone had taken in the shirt to make it smaller," Marie added.

Wyatt looked at Derrick and knew his cousin was thinking the same thing. If the shirt had been altered to fit a smaller person, then the bones probably didn't belong to Willow.

"Anything else you remember about the discovery or found odd?" Wyatt asked.

"Well …" Marie cut her eyes to Nate, who nodded. "It seemed as though the bones were buried with care." A single tear trickled down her cheek. "Like someone cared about whoever had been placed in the ground."

"We're willing to check the area near where the bones were discovered." Nate looked at Marie, who added, "We feel there might be more evidence around the site than what we initially discovered."

Again, Wyatt exchanged a look with Derrick. "Thanks for the offer, but it will be better if my deputies and I conduct a search."

"I don't mean to tell you how to do your jobs," Marie began, "but I would look for something personal that might belong to the bones."

"We will," Wyatt nodded, "and thank you for reaching out with this new information."

"We're glad to help." Nate and Marie followed Wyatt and Derrick back to the front of the store.

"If you think of anything else," Wyatt extended his hand to Marie, then Nate, "please don't hesitate to call."

"Will do." Marie smiled as Derrick plucked another cookie from the plate and stepped outside.

Wyatt tipped his hat, then followed Derrick to his truck. Once inside, he cut his eyes to his cousin.

"What?" Derrick grinned. "I only took two cookies— mine and yours." He took a bite of the second cookie. "And I know you don't like sweets."

Wyatt laughed and exited the bait shop's parking lot. Though the site where the bones were discovered had been explored, Wyatt decided they should expand the search area. He and Derrick would assemble a crew and begin the tedious task of looking for additional clues in Willow's Woods.

CHAPTER EIGHT

The Rocky River Bar had a good lunchtime crowd, and Claire dashed from table to table checking on customers. Dyani headed Harley's way.

"Hi Harley," she smiled. "Here for the champagne?"

Nodding, Harley said, "Surprised to see you here."

"Things are slow at Broken River and Claire had a waitress quit, so I said I'd fill in until she hires someone."

"I'm sure she's glad for the help." Harley gave Claire a wave.

"Claire put the champagne into two boxes and they're behind the bar." Dyani headed toward the hand-carved redwood bar.

A man stood from his stool as they approached, then turned and smiled at Harley.

"This is a nice surprise," Blake Stone said.

"Hi Blake." Harley hoped her shock at seeing Wyatt's brother didn't show on her face. "I didn't know you were in town."

"Blake's moving back to Stoneybrook," Dyani said as she set a box with six bottles onto the bar top.

This time Harley knew her surprise registered in the look she gave him. "Oh, that's great news."

"Can I buy you a beer?" Blake flashed two fingers at Dyani.

"I really have—" Harley began.

"Blake likes the same beer as you." Dyani grabbed glasses from the freezer. "Two Sunrise Surfers coming up."

He pulled a barstool out for her, and Harley took a seat as Dyani placed the beers in front of them.

Blake touched her glass with his, then took a sip. Harley sipped the crisp blonde ale, the malt flavor lingering on her tongue.

"Are you having a party?" Blake angled toward her.

"My friend Busy is coming for a visit. She ordered the champagne." He stared at her with Wyatt's blue eyes and Harley was struck again by how much they looked alike.

"A bottle a day, so she'll be here for twelve days?" Blake smiled.

"You're moving back to Stoneybrook?" Harley countered.

"I investigated Willow Atwood's disappearance with Wyatt." Blake took a long sip from his glass. "When I heard about the newly-discovered remains, I felt a need to come back and help finish the investigation."

"I hope there's finally a resolution." Harley's phone chimed and she looked at a text from Busy.

Busy: *Delay out of SeaTac. Will text from Eugene*

Harley: *K. Safe travels. See you soon*

"All good?" Blake asked.

"Yes. Busy's flight's been delayed." Harley took a sip, wondering if it would be rude to leave without finishing her beer. "Are you still working as a bounty hunter?"

He raised an eyebrow. "I prefer 'fugitive recovery agent'."

"There can't be much need for that type of work in Stoneybrook."

Blake laughed. "I'm also planning to reopen the campground at Willow Lake."

"The campground by Wyatt's lodge?"

When he picked up his glass again, she noticed a slight squint to his eyes. "Wyatt isn't the only Stone in this county."

"Right." Harley reached for her purse and slid off the bar stool. "Good luck with everything."

Blake stood and frowned at the money she placed on the bar. "Beers are on me."

Harley nodded, but didn't pick up the ten-dollar bill. She lifted one box of champagne and turned to leave. As she took a step, her purse strap caught on the back of the stool and she almost pulled it on top of her.

Blake steadied the barstool, then placed his hands on her arms. "Let me carry this for you." He ran his hands along her forearms until they both held the box.

Harley's cheeks warmed when he looked into her eyes. Then, staring past her, his eyes grew dark. A whisper of dread flitted through her gut.

"Wyatt." Stepping back, Blake crossed his arms.

Harley turned slightly and Wyatt took the box from her, returning it to the bar top. He leaned down and covered her lips in a kiss clearly meant to stake his claim.

"Babe." Wyatt smiled at her. "I thought you'd be home waiting on Busy."

The term *babe* took her by surprise, and she could see a flicker of anger in his eyes. "How'd you know I was here?"

He tilted his head and smiled. "Your Lexus is parked in front of the bar." Wyatt waved at Dyani.

"Hey, Chief," Dyani said as she dried her hands on a bar towel. "Luke didn't have any work for me, so I'm helping Claire out. Cool?"

"Yes." Wyatt smiled at her. "Just check in with Luke each night to see if you're needed."

"Will do." Dyani nodded. "Can I get you something?"

"Okay to leave the boxes here while we have lunch?" Wyatt asked.

"Sure." Dyani reached for three menus.

"Just two for lunch." Wyatt took Harley by the hand and headed for a table.

"Wyatt," Blake said, following them. "I know about the recovered bones, the continued search for Willow, and the hunt for Leah's killer. I want to be included in the investigation."

"Come to the station in the morning." Wyatt strode through the restaurant, Harley in tow. She felt like a prize he'd just won at the fair.

When they stopped at a table for four, he pulled a chair out for her. He set his hat onto the table, then sat next to her with his back to Blake.

"Fine." Blake said behind them. "I enjoyed our beer date, Harley."

Wyatt met her eyes, and she opened her lips to protest, but he put a finger on them to silence her.

Harley took his hand in hers. "It wasn't a date."

"I know," he said as Claire approached the table.

"Sorry, Wyatt." She placed glasses of water in front of them. "I wish I could ban him from the bar, but I just can't take sides."

"It's okay, Claire."

"What can I get you two?"

"I'll have the turkey and Swiss," Wyatt said.

"Grilled chicken Caesar for me." Harley smiled at Claire.

"Coming right up," Claire said as she walked away.

"New blouse?" Wyatt ran a fingertip along the neckline of her orange V-neck top, stopping at the top button.

"I might've stopped in at Buckles and Baubles for a minute." She smiled. "Wyatt, I know we agreed not to talk about our past relationships, but ..."

He looked away and drank half his water. When he met her gaze, her heart twinged at the pain she saw in his sky blue eyes.

"Someday, I'll tell you what happened if you really need to know." Wyatt touched her cheek. "For now, though, it's important to me that you don't spend time with Blake."

Dyani delivered their food. The savory smell of Wyatt's French fries floated over Harley, and she snitched a fry. Wyatt smiled, then kissed her.

They both dug into their lunches and Harley thought about how much she loved this man. Her heart ached because he'd been hurt, but she didn't like being caught between two brothers in a war she knew nothing about.

CHAPTER NINE

"I told you not to bring another girl here!" the old crone screamed at him. "We should be packin' up and movin' on now that them bones was found." She wiped her hands on a dirty apron, then resumed stirring her bland beef stew.

He shoved the crying girl toward the young woman, who sported a black eye. Rage boiled within him, and he rushed his mother. "Did you hit her?"

"She was sassin' me, so I showed her who the real boss is." His mother squared her shoulders and jutted out her chin. "Somethin' you'd do well to remember, too."

"If you don't keep your mouth shut," he growled, "I'm going to shut it permanently."

"Oh, big man!" She threw her hands in the air. "And who's going to take care of you, your tramp, her brat, and the crying mess?"

The young woman tried to shush the wailing girl. She took her daughter's hand and huddled in the corner with both children. He glanced at her as she spoke softly to the sobbing young girl.

He turned back to his mother and slapped her across the face. "I'm sick of you and your crap."

She swung at him, and he knocked her to the floor, then proceeded to pummel her with his fists. The rage that had been building within him for years boiled up from his core, and all he could think of was silencing the bitch who had criticized him his whole life. Every punch he landed represented some imperfection she'd labeled him with. He was too stupid to manage a good job. He was too ugly for a pretty girl to love him. He was too damaged to live a normal life.

His knuckles became bloody, and the scent of iron filled his nose. When his mother lie motionless on the grimy kitchen floor, he kicked her with the toe of his boot. She didn't respond.

He looked over his shoulder, noticing the young woman and two girls were missing. He returned his attention to the bloody heap on the floor and bent down to check for a pulse. Nothing.

"Well, it's not like I didn't warn you," he said.

He found it curious he didn't feel sorrow. Instead, he felt relief that the manipulative bitch was dead. Movement behind him caused him to turn. He found the young woman staring at him, fear widening her grey eyes.

"Put the girl in my shed," he picked up his mother's body, "then clean up this mess."

"I-I—" She smoothed her pink tank top. "Maybe you'd like for me to calm you down instead."

He tilted his head and adjusted the dead weight in his arms. "Fine. Feed them and put them to bed. I'll be back in a while."

The young woman had never volunteered herself before and lust flooded his loins as he pushed through the battered screen door. For the first time since he'd taken her from the willow grove, he found himself looking forward to enjoying his captive's willingness all night.

CHAPTER TEN

Harley smiled at her bestie when she stepped from the Uber. The driver made his way to the trunk. Harley bounded down the porch steps just in time for Busy to hand her a briefcase and carry-on from the front passenger seat.

"Traveling light as usual, I see." Harley laughed.

The driver carried two large suitcases onto the porch and set them near the front door. He trudged to the car and opened the back passenger door, then lifted out the last suitcase.

Busy pulled cash from her wallet. "I tipped on the app," she handed him a twenty dollar bill, "but you're such a doll to carry everything to the door."

"My pleasure, ma'am," the driver tipped his baseball cap, "hope you have a nice visit."

"Visit?" Busy laughed. "Oh, Hun, I'm moving to Stoneybrook next month."

"Well, welcome almost-home, then." The driver climbed into his Kia and headed for Little Creek Road.

"Har Har!" Busy hugged her. "I've missed you! And I can't wait to tell you all the gossip from home."

"I've missed you too," Harley headed for the front door, "and I'm guessing gossip will require bevies."

"Did you pick up my order from Claire?" Busy asked as she two-handed a suitcase and carried it inside.

"Yes," Harley grabbed a suitcase too, "and I made a hummus dip to go with your bubbly and my red wine."

"Sounds delicious." Busy brought in the last suitcase. "Is your handsome sheriff coming over tonight?"

"Maybe." Harley avoided eye contact with her bestie. "Why?"

"I was hoping he'd carry my bags upstairs." Busy gathered her briefcase and carry-on from the porch, then closed the door.

Harley walked through the dining room and into the kitchen. She pulled a bottle of champagne from the fridge and set it on the counter next to her red wine. As Busy sauntered in, Harley plucked a wine glass and champagne flute from the cupboard. She poured their drinks and set the glasses onto the drop-leaf table.

Busy carried the hummus dish to the table, then fetched the basket of pita bread from the counter. She took a seat, sipped from her glass, then stared at Harley over the top of her flute.

"What?" Harley took a large sip.

"Why maybe?" Busy dipped a slice of pita into the hummus dip.

"Wyatt's got a lot going on at work." Harley shrugged and dipped a hunk of pita, then popped the bite into her mouth. Stalling, she chewed the creamy garlic dip and toasted pita slowly.

"Uh-huh," Busy raised her eyebrows, her forehead barely wrinkling. "Something happen between you kids?"

"You have gossip from home?" Harley countered.

"Archer's engaged." Busy laughed when Harley spit red wine onto the tabletop.

"To who?" Harley used one napkin to mop her face and another to wipe the table.

"Some Wall Street blonde." Busy took a sip. "She's totally different from you."

"So, my ex-fiancé probably won't cheat on her." Harley drained her glass.

"That's not what I meant." Busy narrowed her eyes. "Seriously, what's going on with you?"

"Noth—" Harley's phone chimed.

"Saved by the bell," Busy emptied her flute, picked up Harley's glass and crossed to the counter.

Wyatt: *Busy arrive safely?*

Harley: *Yes. Still on for dinner at RR?*

Wyatt: *Looking forward to treating my favorite New Yorkers.*

Harley: *Time?*

Wyatt: *Ready when you are, Ms. Harper.*

Harley smiled, then replied: *Finishing a glass of wine, then our way in 15.*

"Wyatt on his way?" Busy placed their glasses onto the table.

"He wants to take us to dinner at Rocky River." Harley took a sip of wine.

"Great," Busy dipped another pita into the hummus, "I had a snack on the plane, but I'm famished."

"I told him we'd be on our way in fifteen minutes." Harley had another hummus laden pita bite. "What's Archer's fiancée like?"

"I hate to say this," Busy took a large sip, "because it gives us blondes a bad rap, but Felicity is ditzy as hell."

"Ditzy and works on Wall Street?" Harley cocked an eyebrow.

"She's some big trader's assistant," Busy drained her flute, "and I think she's latched onto Archer to get away from her lecherous boss."

"So, she's a blonde gold digger?" Harley smiled. "Perfect for Archer."

"The gang seems to like her okay," Busy shrugged, "but I don't spend much time with them anymore." She waggled her empty glass. "Are we drinking or going?"

"Do you want to change or just go?" Harley finished her wine.

"Give me a sec to change into a tank top." Busy stood. "It's too hot for anything with sleeves."

"Okay." Harley laughed. She put the lid on the hummus dish and placed it in the fridge.

When they arrived at Rocky River, Harley smiled at the sight of Wyatt's truck parked in front of the bar. Busy led the way inside and he waved them over. They made their way to the table and Wyatt kissed Harley. He ran a hand through his curly blond locks, and it dawned on Harley that he wasn't wearing his cowboy hat. She loved how sexy he looked with his bangs brushing his forehead. Harley's cheeks warmed when last night's romantic appetizer flashed in her mind.

"Busy," Wyatt hugged her, "welcome back to Stoneybrook."

"Thanks, Wyatt." Busy smiled at them. "I can't wait until I move here!" She looked around. "Now what's a girl gotta do to get a drink in this gin joint?"

"Wyatt ordered for you." Dyani set their drinks onto the table. "Good to see you, Busy."

"You too, and—" Busy began.

"I'll keep em' comin'!" Dyani gave the peace sign over her shoulder and headed back to the bar.

Wyatt pulled out the chair next to him and Harley sat down. Busy took her flute of champagne and headed for Claire and Mercy Edwards. Harley knew her bestie would want to catch up on the Stoneybrook gossip, which flowed daily at Mercy's Babbling Brook Café.

"Thanks for ordering for me," Harley smiled at Wyatt, "but how did you know to order me red wine?" She took a sip.

"Your text said wine …" he tilted his head, "did I get it wrong?"

"No," she kissed him, "you guessed right."

He sipped some beer, and they watched Busy flit from one friend to another.

"Do you think Stoneybrook is ready for Elizabeth Benton?" Harley asked, without looking at him.

"No," Wyatt placed his hand on her thigh, "but I know it will be good for you to have her here."

Wyatt touched her chin, so she'd look at him. His eyes were a lighter blue than usual, and she thought she saw a hint of worry cross his face. He leaned in and kissed her, then touched his forehead to hers.

"Harley, I—"

Before he could say anything, Busy was back with Claire and Mercy. Wyatt brought another chair to the table for Mercy, and everyone sat. Harley was glad Busy was enjoying her first night back in Stoneybrook, but she would've liked to hear what Wyatt had been about to say.

For now, though, she took comfort in the warmth of his hand on her thigh. The sound of his deep laugh when Busy told the story about meeting Archer's fiancée for the first time. And how he looked at her when she spoke, as if he couldn't wait to hear what she had to say.

CHAPTER ELEVEN

The young woman had set the table for his dinner, complete with a napkin under the silverware. After his first bite of stew, he was surprised how flavorful the hearty soup tasted, albeit a touch heavy with garlic. She'd also placed a plate of sliced cucumbers and his usual generic beer on the table.

As he watched her wash the little girl's hands and face, he thought there was something different about the young woman. She seemed calmer. Happier, even.

"Who would like a treat?" she asked, holding two cookies behind her back.

The child jumped up and down, squealing, "Me, me!"

The new girl cut her eyes to him, then took the cookie when the woman handed it to her. Taking their hands, the woman led them to the bedroom she shared with the little girl. After a few minutes, she returned to the kitchen and stood at the end of the table.

"Can I get you anything else?" she asked.

"No," he shook his head, "did you eat?"

"Yes." She gathered his empty dishes and headed to the sink.

"You made the stew taste much better than the old hag's slop." He stood.

"Thank you." She didn't look at him.

He stepped next to her and lifted her chin. "Why did she hit you this time?"

"I-I suggested she add more spices to her cooking," she met his stare, "and she told me to shut the fuck up."

"Well, she won't hit anyone anymore." He touched her black eye. "Does it hurt?"

"No." She shook her head.

"I'm going to take a shower," he kissed her, "wait for me in my room."

She nodded, then returned her focus to washing dishes.

He stood under the spray until the water ran tepid, then dried off and wrapped the towel around his waist. When he stepped into his bedroom, the young woman sat on the end of the bed. She stood as he moved closer.

Even in her simple clothes, she looked beautiful. He kissed her and began unbuttoning her white sleeveless blouse. Slipping the shirt from her shoulders, he covered a breast with his mouth and pulled her closer. He'd always thought her resistance was what drove his lust for her, but desire scorched his loins when she didn't recoil from his touch. He moved to her other breast and lowered her cotton shorts, palming her firm ass.

When he stood back to remove his towel, she stepped from her shorts and moved to the bed. He followed her, sucking in a breath at the sight of her lying naked on the sheets and waiting for him. He lay next to her, caressing her flat stomach, then exploring her body with his mouth. When he reached the edge of her promised land, he thought she lifted her hips in anticipation.

Glancing at her, he found her watching him with narrowed grey eyes. He kissed her luscious mound, then stretched out on top of her. She opened her legs for him, and he slipped into her sweetness. Normally, the young woman would have her eyes closed and her face scrunched in a grimace. Tonight, though, she continued to meet his stare as he set a slow pace. He also noticed something else … she seemed more relaxed, almost welcoming, than she ever had before.

His joy peaked and he laid next to her. She usually bolted from his bed and hid in her room with the little girl, but this time she stayed. He rose up on an elbow and kissed her, then brushed a stray strand of hair from her eyes.

"Would you like for me to stay?" she asked.

He tilted his head. "Yes."

She leaned up and kissed him. "Thank you, Joe, for … for protecting me from your mother."

He knew shock showed on his face. "You're welcome, Willow."

Joe pulled Willow into his arms, and she placed her head on his chest.

For the first time in the five years since he had taken her, the young woman seemed at ease. Joe wasn't sure what to make of Willow's willingness to spend the night with him.

He knew his mother terrorized Willow every chance she got. Still, he thought she'd be afraid of him after he killed his mother.

Maybe Willow was offering herself so he wouldn't harm the girl he'd recently taken. Maybe she was truly thankful he'd finally stood up to his demented mother. Or maybe she wanted to be a willing participant and they'd enjoy each other all night.

A new fire burned within him, and Joe couldn't wait to take Willow again.

CHAPTER TWELVE

Wyatt nodded, and Derrick gave a shrill whistle that echoed through the warm morning air. He then waited for the search crew to turn their attention to him.

"As you all know," Wyatt began, "human remains were found in this area a few days ago." Wyatt cut his eyes to Blake who was walking toward the group, then continued, "The coroner hasn't identified the remains yet, but we have reason to believe they belong to someone other than Willow Atwood."

"Chief," Britt raised his hand, "are we looking for something specific?"

"No." Wyatt narrowed his eyes. His high school friend knew he hated that nickname. "We'd like for you to put anything of interest into a bucket." He pointed toward his truck, where a stack of plastic buckets sat next to a pile of rakes and a box of flashlights. "You've all participated in a grid search before, so let's get started."

"Wait." Derrick held up a hand. "The flashlights might spark something too small to see otherwise. And if you find anything in the ground requiring a shovel, call out so we can do a controlled dig.”

“Also,” Mac began, “there’s a cooler of turkey and ham sandwiches compliments of Mercy. The other cooler has water, so stay hydrated.”

“Any other questions?” Wyatt scanned the crowd. “Let’s get started then.” He followed the crew as they headed for his truck.

“Didn’t expect to see Blake here,” Britt said, catching up to Wyatt.

“It was his case too,” Wyatt responded.

“I remember Leah’s murder was hard on him.” Britt shook his head. “It’s why he gave up his badge, right?”

“He gave up his badge for Ava,” Derrick said as he stepped behind Wyatt.

Wyatt turned and gave his cousin a warning look, then picked up a rake and headed for an area away from everyone else. The sun beat down, but he knew he was sweating into his polo due to his anger at Blake being back in Stoneybrook. What couldn’t his brother have stayed away instead of coming back and dredging up the past.

He tried to focus on the task at hand, but his thoughts jumped to his night with Harley. She’d seemed fine when they’d taken Busy to dinner, and he’d enjoyed hearing her laugh as they sat around the fire drinking her scratch jalapeño margaritas. Wyatt knew he’d hurt her feelings by insinuating she was voluntarily hanging out with Blake. He hadn’t been able to apologize for his behavior at lunch and thought he felt tension between them, so had gone home instead of staying the night. As hard as it had been when Ava ran off with his brother, Wyatt knew he couldn't bear losing Harley. Not to anyone, for any reason.

They'd searched for almost three hours, with everyone taking breaks to eat and drink some water. Wyatt looked out across the area Derrick had identified as the best place to start, estimating they'd searched over half the ground. He'd hoped they'd find a few clues to help identify the recently-discovered bones.

A loud whistle drew everyone's attention. Britt held up a hand. Wyatt and Derrick crossed to Britt, who leaned on a rake. Moving lupine flowers aside with his boot, the scent of honey riding on the breeze, Britt directed his flashlight beam to a spot on the ground. The light sparked a speck of blue lying partially hidden by the ground debris.

"I think it's a toy heart." Britt looked at Wyatt. "When I tried to pick it up, I could tell it's attached to something buried in the ground."

Mac retrieved a shovel and handed it to Wyatt, who inched the dirt away from the object. Once he created a circle, he stuck the nose of the shovel into the ground and lifted a small section of dirt.

Derrick dropped to his knees and sifted through the dirt with his fingers. He gently dusted debris away from what looked like a clump of twigs attached to a blue heart. He nodded as he stood, and Wyatt lifted another shovelful of dirt. He set the clump to the side and repeated the process. When he was about a foot down, the shovel tip struck something hard. Derrick handed the twigs to Britt and hit his knees again. He dug around the object with his hands, then lifted a small skull.

"Jesus, Mary, and Joseph." Mac made the sign of the cross.

Setting the skull aside, Derrick continued digging, stopping when he unearthed a blue blanket. Cradling a decomposed bundle, he came to his feet.

"I have something over here." Blake crouched next to the grave where the hikers had found the first set of bones.

When Wyatt joined him, Blake stood and handed him another bundle of twigs. This bundle had a red heart attached. Wyatt met his brother's stare and wasn't surprised when he bolted to the other side of the grove. Derrick and Wyatt followed Blake, and the three of them scanned the surface for another heart.

"I have it!" Derrick knelt and cleared grass from a third bundle of twigs. Wyatt eased the shovel into the ground and set the clump next to Derrick, who fingered away the debris.

"A pink heart for Leah." Derrick held the small cluster in his palms, then looked at Wyatt. "This is the same type of cross made with willow twigs as the one we think Willow gave to Sadie last year."

CHAPTER THIRTEEN

"I heard you get up early." Busy stepped onto the front porch, cup of coffee in hand. "Did you get any sleep?"

"Some," Harley said and looked at the time on her phone, which showed ten to one.

"What?" Busy sat in the wicker chair next to Harley. "I needed my beauty sleep." She grinned.

Harley took a drink from her water bottle as Busy sipped coffee. They sat looking across the fields.

"Care to tell me what the hell is going on with you and the handsome sheriff?"

Harley shrugged.

"If he's hurt you, he's going to have to answer to me." Busy set her cup down and touched Harley's arm. "What did he do?"

"Nothing." Harley shook her head. "He surprised me yesterday at Rocky River, and found me having a beer with Blake."

"Black sheep brother, Blake?"

"Wyatt was angry," Harley nodded, "and doesn't want me to spend time with Blake."

"Understandable, after he ran off with Wyatt's last girlfriend."

"It bothers me that he thinks I would do the same thing." Harley sipped some water.

"It's also kind of romantic," Busy grinned, "that Wyatt's making it clear he's in love with you and doesn't want to lose you."

"I guess." Harley stood. "It's getting warm, so I'll bring in the horses and check everyone's water. Then we can have a late lunch at the Babbling Brook Café."

"Perfect. I'll jump into some shorts and a tank top while you feed your creatures." Busy stood and headed inside. "And I'd like to stop in at Pebbles and Pretties to talk to Mia about furniture."

Following Busy into the house Harley didn't respond. The lingering scent of burnt toast caused Harley's stomach to growl. She'd tried to eat a second round of toast, but the next piece still tasted bitter, causing her to throw the perfectly-buttered slice into the garbage.

"Har Har," Busy began and Harley faced her. "Jealousy is an evil bitch, but I don't believe Wyatt thinks you'd cheat on him."

"Thanks, Busy." Harley gave her bestie a small smile and headed for the barn.

As she drew close, she could hear Maverick causing a ruckus. Harley walked straight to his stall, eliciting whinnies from Trigger and Elvis. Maverick's breakaway halter had twisted instead of releasing. Now, the damn halter was caught on the new latch Luke had installed. The donkey's large brown eyes were wary, and Harley could see he had a small cut near his jawbone.

"Damn it!" She tried to loosen the halter enough to free Maverick, but the strap was too tangled. She would have to cut the halter.

After she freed him, Maverick tossed his head and stomped around his stall. Speaking in soothing tones, Harley entered slowly. The crazed donkey rushed her. She backpedaled, but not quickly enough. Maverick knocked her down as he bolted from his stall.

"Shit!" she cried when her head hit the ground.

"Are you okay?" Blake asked as he helped her up.

"Yes." Harley tried to step away from him, but swayed on her feet.

Blake swooped her into his arms and strode from the barn, stopping when they came face to face with Wyatt. The look on Wyatt's face made Harley cringe, and she climbed from Blake's arms.

"Wyatt, it's not what you think," she called after him as he stormed toward his truck.

He spun around, his face beet red. "It's exactly what I think." Anger flashed in his eyes before he turned and continued to his truck.

"Don't walk away from me, Wyatt Stone."

He didn't respond, and tears sprang to her eyes when his truck tires spewed gravel as he raced up her driveway. Harley tried to stay on her feet, but crumpled to the ground.

"I've got her," Busy barked at Blake when he tried to help Harley. "Why are you effing here?"

"As soon as we finished the search in Willow's Woods, I came straight here." Blake looked at Harley. "I liked being included by Wyatt, and wanted to apologize for yesterday."

"That worked out well." Busy pulled Harley to her feet. "I need you to leave."

"She hit her head and might have a concussion." Blake headed for his truck.

"She'll be fine." Busy wrapped her arm around Harley's waist and guided her toward the house.

"Nothing happened," Harley mumbled as she stepped into the mudroom.

"I know, sweetie." Busy helped her sit in a chair at the drop-leaf table. "Your sheriff is a man deeply in love, and right now he's letting his jealousy control his behavior."

Busy put an arm around Harley who let her tears flow. "Well, he's being ridiculous because he's not the only one who's deeply in love."

"Yes," Busy held Harley from her, "but you remember our rules, right? Rule number one, boys are stupid—"

"Rule number two," Harley blew her nose, "don't forget rule number one."

"Exactly!" Busy laughed. "Now, do you still feel like going to lunch, cause I'm starving and could use a couple of mimosas!"

"Yes, I think so." Harley stood, but swayed on her feet.

"Maybe we should stay here." Busy pointed to the chair Harley had vacated. "You sit and I'll make us some lunch.

Besides, I have plenty of champagne to make my own mimosas with your cran-raspberry juice."

"Sounds good." Harley tried to nod, but her head pounded with the movement. "Do you remember concussion protocol?"

"Of course," Busy set a bottle of water in front of Harley. "Do you remember the oh-so-fine paramedic who taught the class?"

"I do," Harley managed a smile, "especially the part where he offered to give you mouth-to-mouth if you passed out."

"You don't feel dizzy sitting," Busy scrunched her eyes and tilted her head, "do you?"

"No," Harley didn't try to shake her head, "and I don't feel nauseous. I just have a throbbing headache."

"Okay, good," Busy headed upstairs, "then we'll start with lots of water and some ibuprofen."

Harley sipped water and thought about how it must have looked to Wyatt when he saw her in Blake's arms. Whatever his brother and Ava had done had left a deep wound in her sheriff's heart. Harley hoped she could help Wyatt heal and learn to trust her love for him.

CHAPTER FOURTEEN

"Where the hell have you been?" Joe barked at Willow. Her hair was a tangled mess. There was dirt smudges on her yellow tank top and shorts were dirty too.

"It's a nice afternoon, so I took the girls for a walk." She limped to a chair. "The new girl shoved me down a hill and ran off with my baby." Willow dabbed a rag against a cut on her shin as tears spilled down her cheeks.

"Why'd you take them outside?" Joe ran his hands through his hair. "The cops are crawling all over the field by the lake. It's only a matter of time before they find Mom's body."

"Maybe we should leave," Willow suggested, then stifled a sob.

He stormed across the small room and yanked her to her feet. "You let them go, like the last girl, didn't you?"

"No." She glared at him. "Your new captive knocked me down and ran away with *our* daughter."

Joe gripped her wrist and dragged Willow toward the door. "They're probably lost, so we'll go look for them."

She jerked her arm free. "If we get caught, the police will throw us in jail."

He narrowed his eyes at her. "Why would they arrest you?"

"Because I'm a bad mother." Another round of tears shook Willow's shoulders. "I didn't protect my children, and they'll take my daughter away from me."

Rarely did he feel sorry for her, but the sadness in Willow's eyes made him want to comfort her. The death of the baby boy had been due to his mother's inept midwife skills and Willow had almost died giving birth.

Maybe if they left this hell, they could leave their pasts behind them and start over. Maybe Willow would continue to welcome him in bed. Maybe they could live some semblance of a normal life, far away from the nightmares these hills held for them.

Her lips tasted like raspberry jam and peanut butter when he kissed her, and the scent of grass woven through her hair made him want to hold her until her tears subsided.

"Change out of those dirty clothes and pack a few things." Joe kissed her again, then stepped away. "And we'll leave tonight."

Before he left the shack, he thought he saw a hint of a smile cross her lips. But it didn't matter because they could travel easier without the baggage of his mother, their daughter, and a captive. Willow might have freed the girls, but she'd stayed. And, willing or not, Joe planned to bring her with him into a brighter future.

CHAPTER FIFTEEN

After racing away from Harley's Wyatt had passed out after drinking half of a fifth of single malt. He spent the night on the couch and almost knocked over the bottle sitting on the end table when he stood. He'd been saving the Rogue Spirits Whiskey for a special occasion and anger warmed his cheeks when he remembered why he'd cracked open the bottle.

The vision of Harley in Blake's arms almost made him reach for the whiskey again, but he headed for the kitchen instead. Frankie had made coffee and set a loaf of sliced banana bread next to his favorite cup. He appreciated his cook's efforts. Wyatt popped half a slice of bread into his mouth, filled his cup, then climbed the stairs off the kitchen to his bedroom.

He'd hoped to feel better after a hot shower, but his head still felt fuzzy and his anger at Blake hadn't dissipated. Nor had his embarrassment at storming away from Harley lessened. He wanted to believe nothing was going on between her and Blake, but couldn't shake the fear that he'd lose Harley as he had Ava. And losing Harley would be a far bigger loss.

His phone buzzed and he looked at a text from Derrick: *Come to station ASAP*

Wyatt pulled his gun from the safe in his study, grabbed his keys, and stepped from the house. He inhaled the scent of freshly cut hay, glad he'd opted for a short-sleeved cotton button down, given the day was already warm. The bright morning sunshine caused his eyes to squint and his head to pound.

"It's going to be a long day," he muttered, climbing into his truck. Since his hair was still wet, he placed his hat on the seat. He plucked his sunglasses from the dash and slipped them on.

When he parked at the station, he found Derrick pacing in front of the open doors.

"The new set of bones are a baby boy. And we have a partial fingerprint on the blue heart. The blanket still showed a stain, which the lab thinks is amniotic fluid." He took a breath, then continued, "And—"

"Derrick." Wyatt placed a hand on his cousin's shoulder. "Let's go inside."

Derrick nodded and led the way. Blake, along with Simms and Barnes, stood near the coffee pot. They formed a semi-circle as Wyatt and Derrick joined them.

Wyatt looked at Derrick. "I'm guessing the lab can get DNA from the blanket."

"Yes—revealing both parents." He flashed a smile. "I think it's time to alert the FBI to our new discoveries."

"You've already called them, right?" Wyatt returned Derrick's smile when he nodded.

"There isn't a fingerprint on file for Willow," Blake said, and Wyatt glanced at him before reaching for the coffee pot. "But it could be useful if we find her bod—"

"She's a survivor." Derrick shook his head. "She's alive. And we're going to find her."

"Anything else discovered in the search?" Wyatt asked.

"No, Chief." Simms coughed. "CSU is still sorting through the buckets, but nothing so far."

The station phone rang, and Barnes picked up the closest receiver. "Sheriff's Department." He waved at Wyatt and handed him the phone.

"Sheriff Stone." Wyatt listened, then met the circle of questioning gazes. He disconnected and said, "Two young girls have been found wandering the shore of Willow Lake."

Derrick bolted outside and jumped into Wyatt's truck. Before he could object, Blake settled onto the backseat. Derrick hit a button, and the siren wailed as they headed out of Stoneybrook toward the lodge at Willow Lake.

CHAPTER SIXTEEN

Harley had run the gamut of emotions as Busy kept her company throughout the night. Her bestie offered many logical reasons why Sheriff Stone hadn't called, but Harley worried their relationship might be over. If Wyatt didn't love her enough to trust she wouldn't run off with his brother, then he probably didn't love her at all. Maybe she should throw in the towel and go back to Manhattan.

When she told Busy she wanted to sell the ranch and move back to New York, her bestie bristled and narrowed her eyes at Harley.

"Harley Quinn Harper," Busy had wagged a finger at her, "I'm sticking to my plan to move to Stoneybrook in a month. Running away isn't an option."

"But what if Wyatt's not ready for a relationship?" Harley swiped tears from her eyes. "What if he's not over Ava? What if we moved too fast and we're not in love, just in lust?"

"I think all this worrying is a result of you hitting your head." Busy took a drink from her flute. "Here's an idea, what if the two of you practice what your Aunt Cindy used to tell everyone and just 'shut up and love' each other!"

Harley had laughed, the effort causing her head to throb. Busy's giggling sent her to the bathroom off the mudroom before she wet her pants. Then the two friends had stayed up until the wee hours of the morning reminiscing about Aunt Cindy and her words of wisdom.

When she woke this morning, Harley had a slight headache and dark circles under her eyes. And despite staying up and laughing with Busy, Harley still felt sad. She knew Wyatt was probably busy at work, but she couldn't shake the feeling their hot and heavy romance had flamed out.

Harley made an extra strong pot of hazelnut coffee and now sat on the front porch. Her Aunt Cindy's smiling face flashed in her mind, and she could almost hear her weighing in on Harley's current relationship woes.

"Why are you jumping to conclusions?" Aunt Cindy would ask. "You don't know what's kept your sheriff from calling you." Then she would laugh. "You know, Harley, winning over the grouchy ones has always been my favorite thing to do! You should give it a try." With a knowing look she would dispense some pearl of wisdom like, "Forgive Wyatt because he's your person and you're in love with him."

Harley took a sip of coffee, deciding it couldn't hurt to try to be more like her beloved Aunt Cindy. She would see the good in people and … 'shut up and love.'

Once her creatures were fed and watered for the day, Busy insisted they drive into Stoneybrook for breakfast at the Babbling Brook Café. Harley had to admit it felt good to abandon her pity party and enjoy the beautiful day.

"More coffee?" Mercy stood at the counter, carafe hovering over their cups.

"Yes, thanks." Harley smiled at her.

"Did you hear the latest?" Mercy asked. "Deputy Simms told me this morning a female body was found near the willow grove."

"Do they know who she is?" Harley prayed it wasn't Willow Atwood.

"No," Mercy shook her head, "Simms said it's an older woman. When I asked if he thought she was connected to the search for Willow, he declined to speculate. But it does seem odd, right?"

"Odd's an understatement," Busy replied.

"And I heard Wyatt's headed to Willow Lake, but no one knows why," Mercy added.

Harley tried to channel her Aunt Cindy's positive attitude, but still flinched at the mention of Wyatt's name. She hadn't heard from him since he'd sped away from the Redneck Ranch yesterday afternoon. Her only connection to Wyatt had been a visit from Luke when he returned Maverick to her this morning.

"Your breakfast okay, Hun?" Mercy pointed to Harley's half-eaten veggie omelet.

"Yes, just not hungry." Harley attempted a smile.

"Mercy," Busy said, pushing her empty plate away. "Can you fix us a couple of your summer crush mimosas?"

"Sure, Hun." Mercy turned toward the back counter. "Are you celebrating something?"

"Yes!" Busy grinned. "I'm moving to Stoneybrook!"

"That's great news!" Mercy set their drinks in front of them. "Are you two going to the dance Friday night?"

Harley shook her head, but Busy responded with, "We wouldn't miss it."

As they drove back to Harley's ranch, Busy insisted they stop by Buckles and Baubles to pick out new outfits for the dance.

The owner, Kaye Norman, was Claire's sister. She smiled when they stepped inside the beautifully decorated clothing store.

"What brings you two in today?" Kaye straightened western blouses on a rounder.

"We need new outfits for the dance on Friday." Busy made a beeline for a rack of summer dresses.

"Perfect timing," Kaye said, "I just received new inventory. Now what are you thinking, a dress or a skirt?"

Harley partially listened to her bestie and Kaye discussing outfits for the Memorial Day dance. With any luck, Harley would come up with a reason to skip the festivities and stay home.

CHAPTER SEVENTEEN

Wyatt was glad to be home after being gone for four days. He was exhausted from the whirlwind task of reuniting the kidnapped girl with her very grateful parents. Despite the light Saturday afternoon traffic, the hour-long drive from Salem seemed longer. They kept thanking him for rescuing their fourteen year-old daughter, and Wyatt had wished he could explain their gratitude was owed to Willow Atwood.

He assumed Willow had managed to set the fourteen year-old and her daughter, Cedar, free as she had done with Sadie last year. His FBI friend, Agent Finn Carter, had met him at the State Police offices even though this girl hadn't been transported across state lines. Finn, and his partner, Agent Mike Daniels, were listed as the agents of record on Sadie's kidnapping case, so Finn wanted to be kept apprised of any new developments.

They still didn't have a name for Willow's kidnapper. However, the young girl did report that the man who took her didn't hurt her. That a nice woman took care of her and baked her cookies. That she played with a little girl who was about four. And, something interesting … the man had hit a mean old woman, who then stopped yelling. Wyatt wondered if this woman could be the body recently found south of the willow grove. It was possible the female body had been related to Willow's kidnapper. Something to follow up on once the body was identified.

Wyatt opened the fridge to see what leftovers Frankie had tucked inside. He pulled out a dish of lasagna and a beer, then carried the container to the stove. After plating a piece, he set the plate into the microwave and pushed reheat. While the lasagna warmed, he cracked open the Coor's Light and checked his phone.

The first text was from Derrick, and Wyatt smiled.

Derrick: *The dance is at 7. Be sure to change. Try not to be late.*

Wyatt: *Just arrived BR. Will try my best to be on time.*

He frowned at a text from his half-sister, the mayor.

Ria: *Heard you're back. Let's meet to discuss Atwood investigation.*

Wyatt: *Sure. Next week*

He knew Ria was just as concerned about finding Willow as the rest of them, but he still dreaded having his case scrutinized. Wyatt felt she had self-serving motivations for knowing the minutia of the investigation.

The next text was from Blake. Neither of them had mentioned the incident at Harley's, and Wyatt hadn't talked to his brother after he left for Salem. Blake had wanted to come to Salem too, but Wyatt reminded him he wasn't currently an official deputy sheriff for Stone County.

Blake: *Nothing new at the station. Talk soon.*
Wyatt: *Copy*

He hoped Blake wouldn't come to the Memorial Day dance at the Rocky River Bar. If he did, Wyatt would focus on keeping his temper in check.

He was disappointed that he didn't have a text from Harley. But could he blame her for not reaching out? He'd assumed the worst about her and Blake. Harley had a right to be angry with him. For a minute he considered texting her to see if she'd like a ride, then he thought about her saying no thank you. Maybe he'd stand a better chance at forgiveness if he showed up *hat in hand* at the dance.

When the microwave dinged, he lifted his plate out. He peeked inside the bread box and smiled at a plastic bag of garlic bread. Seated at the kitchen table, he forked in some lasagna and washed it down with a swig of beer.

"Hey, Chief," Luke said, "thought I heard your truck."

"Just got back." Wyatt pointed at his plate. "You hungry?"

"No," Luke shook his head, "wanted to check in before Hannah drags me to the dance."

"Everything good here?" Wyatt took another bite.

"Yes. Dave and Jack left for the circuit, so Dyani's been splitting her time between here and Rocky River." Luke crossed to the fridge and grabbed a beer. "Everything's good at Harley's too."

"Thanks for keeping an eye on her place while I was gone." Wyatt smiled.

"You can thank Maverick," Luke laughed, "he was the perfect excuse to go by the Redneck Ranch a couple of times."

Wyatt took a large sip of beer and held Luke's questioning stare. "What?"

"I know I'm not a relationship expert," Luke took a drink, "but you need to let go of your anger at Blake. Maybe even forgive him."

"Because?" Grabbing another beer, Wyatt leaned against the counter next to the fridge.

"You know why." Luke headed toward the utility room. "Your anger is clouding your logic when it comes to Harley."

"I'm not going to forgive him," Wyatt called after Luke.

"Fine!" Luke shouted back. "But at least stop letting your bitterness toward Blake bleed into your relationship with Harley."

"Fine!" Wyatt snapped.

He drained his beer and headed upstairs to his bedroom. Luke was right. He wasn't a relationship expert; he'd just happened to marry one of the sweetest girls in Stoneybrook, and she put up with his sorry ass. Wyatt turned on the shower and stepped under the hot spray. Of course, Luke also might be right about Wyatt and his inability to control his anger at Blake for running away with Ava.

When he stepped from his closet, Wyatt assessed his outfit. He slipped on the blue button-down shirt Harley had given him for their one year anniversary. She said the color made his eyes a darker blue. And of course, he wore Levi's with his new black Lucchese boots. He dabbed on Cowboy cologne—another gift Harley had given him. The woody, sage scent conjured an image of them lying in each other's arms. Wyatt grabbed his black cowboy hat, crucial to the *hat in hand* scenario, and headed downstairs.

Maybe, if he was lucky, Harley would accept his apology and give him a chance to do better. Maybe he should tell her about being devastated when Ava ran off with Blake. Maybe the beautiful owner of the Redneck Ranch would say his past didn't matter—and she loved him regardless of his wounded heart.

CHAPTER EIGHTEEN

After feeding her creatures and putting salve on Maverick's wound, Harley had showered and dressed in her new outfit from Buckles and Baubles. The tight jean skirt and red low-cut, sleeveless blouse went perfectly with her new dark red Ropers. If she had to go to the effing Memorial Day dance, then she wanted Wyatt Stone, if he showed, to notice what he'd walked away from.

"You ready?" Busy called from the kitchen.

Harley sprayed a touch of Cowgirl Secrets, a gift from Wyatt, on her wrists. The hint of jasmine brought tears to her eyes. She blinked to clear them away as she added diamond studs to her ears and bloodred lipstick to her lips. She took one last look in the mirror, then headed downstairs.

"Damn, girl." Busy whistled. "If Wyatt wasn't sorry for storming off, he will be now."

"You look fabulous, too." Harley pointed at Busy. Her new brown jersey dress featured turquoise piping and a fringed skirt. "Hoping to see Ace at the dance?"

"Only if he arrives without his girlfriend." Busy grinned.

As they drove to Stoneybrook, Busy prattled on about her move from New York, but Harley's mind couldn't let go of a singular thought: *How was she going to react if Wyatt actually came to the dance? Angry? Sad? Joyful?*

They had to park up the block from Rocky River, and Busy complained about having to walk that far in her new turquoise boots. She opened one side of the large double doors and Harley turned away, intent on running back to her car.

"Come on, Har Har," Busy took her hand and led her inside, "we both need a night of fun!"

"Welcome, lovelies," Claire, dressed in a blouse from her sister's shop and a pair of Wranglers, greeted them with hugs. "You two look stunning."

Scanning the bar for Wyatt, Harley didn't realize she'd been holding her breath until Claire said, "Your sheriff's not here." She motioned for them to follow her. "I think we could use a shot of tequila."

Dyani, who wore a white leather headband with white feathers hanging down the back of her long jet black hair, grabbed a bottle of Herradura. She poured four shots, then lifted one in toast.

"What?" she said to Claire. "I'm only having one, and you know it's been a difficult few days."

Harley wondered about Dyani's comment. Once she held her shot, though, she forgot her concern.

"To life getting back to normal in Stoneybrook and at Broken River." Dyani tossed down her shot, held Harley's stare for a beat, then moved down the bar to help another customer.

"Wyatt's been in Salem helping the state police locate the kidnapped girl's parents and meeting with the FBI about Willow." Claire sipped some tequila. "And according to Dyani, a couple of ranch hands left for the rodeo circuit, so Luke's running the ranch shorthanded."

"What about the other little girl?" Busy asked. "Is Bonnie still taking care of her?"

"It's actually been a group effort," Claire began, "the whole town has been taking turns sitting with her, bringing her clothes and toys like we did for Sadie."

"The girl's been asking for her Aunt Cedar, and her grandparents are on their way from Nevada," Derrick said behind them. "But Echo isn't ready to meet her namesake niece."

"Hi, Derrick." Harley smiled at him. "You look very handsome."

He touched the silver horseshoe clasp of his bolo tie. "And you look nice, too." Derrick looked past her, then met her eyes. "Wyatt misses you."

Without waiting for a reply, he headed toward a table where Blake and the other deputies were seated. Blake met her stare and Harley looked away.

"I love this song!" Busy grabbed Harley's hand and headed for the dance floor. It took Harley a beat to realize the song was Lainey Wilson's "Smell Like Smoke." She cocked an eyebrow.

"What?" Busy said, gyrating to the music. "I'm moving here, so I'm learning all things country."

Laughing, Harley found her rhythm. Ace joined them, without a girlfriend in tow. After the past few days of solitude, it felt good to laugh and be with friends.

A hand at her waist caused Harley to turn. She found Wyatt Stone searching her eyes with an intense blue stare. Her breath caught in her throat, and she couldn't find her voice. Holding his hat in his hands, he leaned close to her ear and whispered, "Forgive me?"

Harley saw concern in his eyes, and tears sprang to hers as she nodded.

"You and me." He kissed her, then placed a hand on her cheek. "From now on, it's just *us*." Harley moved closer to him, and Wyatt pulled her into his arms. She twined her hands around his neck, and he leaned down to kiss her again. "No matter what."

The song shifted to Eric Church's "You Make It Look So Easy" and Wyatt guided her around the dance floor. He looked into her eyes, holding her against him, moving with the rhythm. As the melody floated from the speakers, Harley had to agree with the song. There might be days when she and Wyatt wanted to quit. But, as her Aunt Cindy would expect of her, Harley planned to 'shut up and love' her handsome sheriff. She'd do everything she could to make their love easy. And, hopefully, they would have a love that lasted a lifetime.

WHISPERING WILLOWS

 THE END

ACKNOWLEDGEMENTS

Though heartfelt, my simple "thank you" seems lacking when acknowledging my team of Beta Readers: Cindy Schmid, Gina Greb, Mary Eastman, Sharon North, and Stacy Robinson, who bolster my confidence with kind words of praise. A huge thank you to Joyce Wise, Editor, who makes sure the errors I miss are found and corrected before publishing. These women dedicated endless hours and offered excellent suggestions to help WHISPERING WILLOWS become a mystery with some answers and more questions. Their combined eye for detail always makes me a better writer.

DISCLOSURES

My team and I made every effort to ensure this novel is error free. But we're human, so please accept our apologies for any mistakes you may find. Should you uncover errors while enjoying WHISPERING WILLOWS, please feel free to email me at: author.kimilakay.com

ABOUT THE AUTHOR

Kimila Kay lives in Donald, Oregon with her husband, Randy, and a feisty black cat, Halle. She is currently a member of Northwest Independent Writers Association (NIWA), Ladies of Mystery, Sisters in Crime, Willamette Writers, and Windtree Press.

Her cross-cultural series, Mexico Mayhem, includes "Peril in Paradise", "Malice in Mazatlán" and "Vanished in Vallarta." Still planned for the series are "Chaos in Cabo" (Fall/2024), "Lost in Loreto" and "Fiasco in Peñasco."

The Stoneybrook Mysteries series includes "Redneck Ranch", "Five Golden Rings" and "Whispering Willows". "Willow's Woods" will be available in summer of 2024. "Rattlesnake Ravine" will be available spring of 2025 and "Fatal Falls" is planned for summer of 2025.

You can learn more about Kimila through her blog posts on her website - KimilaKay.com, Ladies of Mystery - ladiesofmystery.com, and Windtree Press - windtreepress.com.

WILLOW'S WOODS

KIMILA KAY

CHAPTER ONE

The past month had been the calmest of his life. Without the extra baggage of his mother and their daughter, he and Willow had settled into an easy routine.

Willow seemed to have accepted her fate knowing their daughter, Cedar, was now safe. Joe hated the idea that Willow thought he'd hurt the child, but if he was being honest with himself, did he know for sure he wouldn't hurt the little girl?

And though Willow had returned to rejecting his advances, their sexual escapades had quieted the dark animal lurking within his soul. *For now*, he thought.

Joe had avoided returning to Oregon and kept their travel to northern California. Living on the run had stretched his meager savings, and he knew he'd have to find a menial job soon. They always stayed in cheap motels and ate burgers or Chinese in their room. Recently, he'd splurged on a cute bungalow style motel right on the beach in Crescent City. Willow had sat for an hour in a chair by the large picture window, staring at the blueish-green water of the undulating Pacific Ocean.

Joe had treated her to dinner at a dive seafood restaurant where they'd enjoyed shrimp scampi and clam chowder. He'd told her he liked her hair, which she'd curled, and that she looked pretty.

Willow, dressed in a pink cotton nightgown and smelling slightly of garlic butter, came to him that night, as she had done the night he'd killed his mother.

After they had made love, she'd kissed his cheek and said, "Thank you for dinner, Joe."

And that's when Joe knew. He either had to kill Willow Atwood or let her go. Despite his evil alter ego laying low the past month, he feared the desire to have a new young thing could flare up at any time.

But the main reason for ending his time with Willow was because he'd fallen in love with the young girl he'd abducted five years ago.

CHAPTER TWO

Wyatt Stone still hadn't adjusted to his younger brother being back in Stoneybrook. Standing at the station's check-in counter, Wyatt poured stale coffee into a chipped mug and looked at Blake who sat at his old desk.

The other deputies had accepted Blake back, understanding he would continue to be part of the Willow Atwood investigation. His brother had assigned himself the task of searching the internet for reports of missing girls, hoping for a lead to connect Willow's abductor to a new disappearance. It surprised Wyatt how the deputies, even Derrick, acted like no time had passed since Blake had left Stoneybrook with Ava Parker over eighteen months ago.

Wyatt's cheeks warmed and Blake looked at him as if he knew his thoughts. His brother lowered his gaze and Wyatt assumed the anger he still felt had shown on his face.

His phoned buzzed. He smiled at Harley's name, reminding him who was important in his life now.

Harley: *Hi. Lunch still?*

Wyatt: *Hi. Yes. RRB or BBC?*

Harley: *Rocky River. Picking up Busy's champagne order*

Wyatt: *See you in thirty*

Harley responded with the kissing emoji, so Wyatt texted back the same reply. When he looked up, Blake was watching him. That's when he realized his anger wasn't because Blake had ran off with Ava. It stemmed from concern his brother would try to do the same with Harley.

"Hey, Chief," Simms said as he stepped to the counter. "A California statie found an abandoned vehicle on the 101 highway." Simms handed Wyatt a traffic report. "Sounds like the engine seized up."

Wyatt took the sheet from his deputy. "This could be the car Sadie described as stinking and burning her eyes. Probably ran out of oil."

"Yep." Simms produced a printout of a map. "The Ford Escape was found here, near Crescent City. I have the local police checking all the hotels, restaurants, grocery stores, the usual." He looked at Wyatt. "And asked for a list of items from the car."

"Any reports of stolen cars nearby?" Wyatt asked.

"Nothing yet." Simms headed back to his desk.

Wyatt sipped the hours old coffee and cringed. "Keep me posted." He headed for the small kitchen area and emptied his cup. When he turned toward his office, he found Derrick standing behind him.

"Derrick." Wyatt waited for his autistic cousin to look at him.

"A Chevy Malibu was reported abandoned in Cave Junction." Derrick turned and headed for the chalkboard. He'd taped maps of California and Oregon on one side so they could track Willow and her abductor's possible locations.

Derrick placed a yellow star next to the town's name. He'd come up with the colored star system: yellow for cars, blue for motels, green for thefts, and red for actual sightings. He also used orange for sightings at new grocery stores. Brown stars indicated stores from the receipts Willow had stashed in the wall of the shack they'd found last year in a ravine.

Derrick assigned purple stars to represent missing children, but so far Blake had not found any recent reports of abductions. The map was a kaleidoscope of color but had yet to produce any actionable leads.

"Did Simms tell you about the car found in Crescent City?"

Derrick nodded and placed another yellow star on the map. "I think the abandoned Malibu was stolen from Crescent City."

"Possibly." Wyatt scanned the map. "Do you have a list of items recovered from the Malibu?"

"Not yet." Derrick smiled. "But I did inform the Josephine County Sheriff's department that Willow likes to hide clues."

"She might not have had time to hide anything in the Chevy." Wyatt studied the map as Blake joined them.

"So, two abandoned cars on roads leading to Oregon," he said. "Think our guy's bringing Willow back to Stoneybrook?"

"Maybe, but I don't think he's following his old routes." Derrick tapped the map, then touched a brown star. "There have been no new sightings at these locations."

"Derrick," Deputy Barnes barked, "Josephine County Sheriff's for you." He placed the call on hold as Derrick headed for his desk.

"Wyatt," Blake said.

Wyatt watched Derrick pick up the call and wished he'd followed him to his desk. He cut his eyes to his brother.

"I thought maybe we could grab a beer." Blake held Wyatt's stare.

"Blake," Wyatt placed his hands on his hips, "you may be back temporarily, but we still have nothing to discuss."

"You might have nothing to discuss," Blake's tone had an edge, "but I have plenty to say, so you can just listen."

Wyatt resisted the urge to punch Blake in the mouth.

"I'm not interested in anything you have to say." Wyatt turned to leave, and Blake grabbed his forearm.

"You can hate me as much as you want, brother. But I'm not leaving Stoneybrook." Blake released Wyatt's arm. "And I'm planning to reopen the campground by *our* lodge, so we need to find a way to get along."

Wyatt gritted his teeth. Now wasn't the time to get into a pissing match with his brother over the ownership of the lodge. But Blake no longer had any claim to the lodge or campground, a fact Wyatt knew Blake would fight to change.

"I know finding Willow is important to you, so you can stay until the investigation is closed." Wyatt turned toward his cousin who had ended his call. "Then you *are* leaving Stoneybrook." Wyatt headed for Derrick who was tapping the keys on his laptop.

"Anything new?" Wyatt asked as he approached.

"A Cave Junction individual reported his Kia Sportage stolen and has offered a reward for a briefcase left on the backseat."

"And?" Wyatt followed Derrick back to the chalkboard where Blake and the other deputies had gathered.

"According to the report, the briefcase contains a laptop and credit cards." Derrick added a green star to the map next to the town's name, then looked at Wyatt, his eyes an electric blue. "I think there's cash in the briefcase, because the owner has offered a five thousand dollar reward."

"Or maybe he has valuable info on the computer," Barnes speculated.

"No." Derrick shook his head, his tone an octave higher than before. "He probably has his files backed up to the Cloud and he can buy a new laptop for under two grand."

"Cave Junction still has illegal marijuana growers, maybe the laptop contains names of potential buyers or sellers," Blake said, "the list could be on the laptop and in the cloud.

Derrick looked at Wyatt and he knew his cousin was weighing whether Blake's point was valid. The best thing to do was to distract Derrick with a task so he wouldn't obsess over Blake's suggestion.

"Derrick." Wyatt waited for him to make eye contact. "Press the Josephine County Sheriff to expedite the search of the Malibu."

Derrick narrowed his eyes at Blake, then marched to his desk.

"Simms," Wyatt said. "It's unlikely our perp would try to pawn a laptop, but let's check pawn shops within a sixty mile radius."

"Copy, Chief." Simms headed for his desk.

"Barnes." Wyatt checked the time on his watch. "If the briefcase was full of cash, then maybe our guy buys another car or makes a different large purchase."

"Yep, I'm on it," Barnes called as he walked to his desk, "I'll check dealerships, car lots, and big box stores."

Wyatt turned and strode toward the station doors.

"Guess I'll follow up on the illegal marijuana angle," Blake said as Wyatt exited the station.

Wyatt climbed behind the wheel of his Silverado, cranked the engine, and exited the parking lot. The day had warmed more than predicted and he switched on the air conditioning. After a few minutes, the cab of his truck cooled, but Wyatt's blood still ran hot. If only Blake would just leave town.

After the short drive to Rocky River Bar, Wyatt parked at the curb behind Harley's Lexus. His pulse quickened at the thought of seeing her. When he stepped through the already open double doors, he smiled at the sight of Harley talking to Claire Norman. He loved how Harley tilted her head, laughing at something Claire had said. Loved how cute she looked in a white, sleeveless blouse, denim skirt and Ropers. He pushed the tail of his Stone County Sheriff's polo into his Levi's waistband, wishing he worn a nicer shirt.

Harley tucked a strand of dark hair behind her ear and turned to look at him. Wyatt smiled and was sure he looked like a teenager on his first date. He closed the distance to meet her at the bar.

"Hi." He kissed her, the scent of lemongrass enveloping him.

"Hi." She smiled and placed her hand on his chest.

"You two want your usual table?" Claire headed to the table for four she'd designated as their spot.

Wyatt took Harley's hand and followed Claire. He pulled out a chair for Harley, then sat in the seat across from her. He took off his hat and set it on the table.

Claire tapped her order pad with a pen. "Having your usuals or something different today?"

"Usual for me," Harley said.

"I think I'll have the rock fish tacos too." Wyatt smiled at Claire.

"And water for Wyatt, a Sunrise Surfer for Harley," Claire said as she headed for the bar.

"How boring are we?" Harley laughed.

Wyatt raised from his chair, leaned across the table, and covered her lips with his. "Nothing about you is boring, Ms. Harper." He kissed her forehead before he sat back in his chair.

Harley's cheeks bloomed red as she asked, "How's your Friday been?"

He knew his frustration with Blake showed on his face when she cocked an eyebrow.

"Blake?" Harley asked as Dyani Belle delivered his water and her beer.

"Harley," Dyani said. "Busy's order is ready. Want me to put the cases in your trunk?"

"That would be great." Harley handed Dyani her keys.

Wyatt stood. "I'll give you a hand."

"I've got it, Chief," Dyani headed back to the bar, "the boxes weigh less than a bale of straw."

Wyatt was still frowning at the moniker Chief when Harley said, "You should just embrace the nickname." She grinned. "By the way, I missed waking up next to you."

"Is that all you missed?" Wyatt returned her grin.

"Well, I did miss being tucked in too."

Dyani stepped into the bar and glanced at Wyatt as Claire hurried to the open doors. She waved her hands at someone and when Wyatt saw the intruder, dread snaked through his stomach.

"Wyatt?" Harley touched his arm.

"Harley," he took her hand in his, "I'm sorry."

"Wyatt," Ava Parker said as she approached their table, "it's so good to see you." She sat in the chair next to him.

Claire stood at the table; her face mottled with anger. "Your food is coming." She gave Wyatt a headshake, then held her hands palms up.

"Thanks, Claire." Wyatt looked at Harley, then glared at Ava. "Why are you here?"

"Oh, so many reasons." She touched the scar on his upper lip, just above his mustache. "What happened?"

Wyatt leaned away from her. "Answer the question, Ava."

"Sally called to see if I wanted to sell my mom's house." Ava placed her hand on his arm. "Evidently, Stoneybrook is being invaded by New Yorkers."

Harley flinched and tried to pull her hand free of his.

"Wyatt, where are your manners?" Ava extended her hand to Harley. "Ava Parker, Wyatt's ..." she glanced at him, "friend."

"Ava, this is Harley Harper," Wyatt let go of Harley's hand so she could shake Ava's. "She's the owner of the Redneck Ranch and a friend of mine."

As soon as the words came out of his mouth, he wished he could swallow them. He knew he should've introduced Harley as his girlfriend.

"It's nice to meet you." Harley pushed her chair back, stood, and offered the smile he knew she hid behind when she was angry. "I need to deliver Busy's champagne, so I'd better be on my way."

"Ah, it's your friend who bought the house next to my mom's place." Ava's smile didn't reach her eyes.

"Yes," Harley nodded as Wyatt stood also, "I'm the other New Yorker."

"Well, it's nice to meet the new owner of my family's ranch," Ava said, a hint of annoyance in her tone.

"I'll walk you out," Wyatt said as Dyani delivered their tacos.

"No need." Harley handed Dyani forty dollars. "Enjoy your lunch date. My treat." Harley looked at Wyatt, anger sparking the gold flecks in her amber eyes, then turned and walked away.

Dyani shook her head at him, then left him alone with the woman who broke his heart, wishing he hadn't hurt the one who made him fall in love again.

CHAPTER THREE

As she rushed from the bar, Harley's emotions ping ponged between being confused, hurt, and angry. She clicked the locks on her Lexus and climbed behind the wheel. She moved the gear shifter and punched the gas, startled when the car jumped backwards. The sickening thud registered in her brain, and she knew she'd backed into Wyatt's truck.

Tears poured down her cheeks as she switched out of reverse and pulled from the curb. When she passed the Rocky River Bar's open doors, she saw Wyatt waving for her to stop and heard him calling her name.

Harley wanted to go back to the Redneck Ranch and lock herself inside her old farmhouse. Instead, she headed for Busy's new home. Another wave of tears blurred her vision and she swiped at her eyes. Harley had been excited about Busy moving to Stoneybrook. Now, though, she realized how grateful she was to have her bestie close by.

Her phone chimed and she glanced at the screen which showed a text from Wyatt.

Wyatt: *Call me*

Next, she saw an incoming call from him, which Harley ignored. Her mind raced with questions. *Why hadn't he introduced her as his girlfriend? Why hadn't he told her about his exe's return to Stoneybrook? Why didn't he tell the bitch who broke his heart to eff off?*

Of course, as it always did, her imagination took the negative thoughts, weaving them into ugly scenarios. *Wyatt was glad to see his old flame and embarrassed to introduce Harley as his girlfriend. Wyatt was still in love with Ava and that's why he'd been hesitant to tell Harley what she already knew— that the redhead had run away with his brother and broke Wyatt's heart.*

She parked in the driveway, exited her car, and headed for the front porch. Busy held the screen door open for her and Harley stepped inside.

"Wyatt called," Busy hugged Harley, "and wants you to call him back."

She handed Harley a tissue box and headed for the kitchen located at the back of her house. The windows of the nook were open, and the powdery floral scent of lilacs drifted in on a warm breeze. Busy poured them each a glass of cabernet. She placed the glasses on a vintage red and white Formica table, then sat in a matching chair.

Harley sat too, blew her nose, and held her friend's light blue stare. "I'm not calling him back."

"He said Ava Parker blindsided you two at lunch."

Harley nodded, then took a sip of wine.

"I'm guessing having Wyatt's ex show up was unpleasant," Busy began and circled her finger at Harley, "but what's behind the tears?"

"He introduced me as his *friend*." Harley covered her face with her hands.

Busy reached out and touched her arm. "And you're upset because he didn't say girlfriend?"

Harley blew her nose again and looked at another text from Wyatt.

Wyatt: *Harley, please call me or come to the station*

"I don't think your handsome sheriff sees you as just a friend," Busy said, "and I think he considers you way more than a girlfriend."

Harley sipped some wine, then studied Busy over the top of her glass.

"Now tell me what this bitch Ava looks like." Busy took a drink.

Harley shrugged. "She's beautiful."

"Bullshit," Busy shook her head, "I'm sure she has flaws we can make fun of so spill."

"She's a redhead, with greenish-gray eyes and a perfect figure."

"Natural redhead or bad dye job?"

A slight smile curved Harley's lips. "Now that you mention it, her hair color does seem kind of brassy."

"And you know there's no such thing as a perfect body." Busy stood and did a pirouette. "It takes a lot of effort to make all of this," she ran her hands down the sides of her sleeveless denim romper, "look gorgeous."

A laugh escaped Harley's lips, but then she frowned. "Ava Parker's mom owns the house next door."

"And Ava's come to town to sell the place?" Busy took a sip.

"Possibly." Harley's phone chimed and she looked at a text from Dyani, then continued, "realtor Sally told Ava Stoneybrook is being invaded by New Yorkers."

"That's not very nice." Busy raised her perfectly sculpted eyebrows, almost creasing her smooth forehead. "Sally must still be pissed I bought this place after the Gilman's didn't renew their listing with her."

"Probably." Harley nodded. "Ava's staying next door while she's in Stoneybrook."

Busy grinned. "That could make things interesting."

"Busy," Harley tilted her head, "what are you planning?"

"For starters," Busy stood, "we need to get our asses in gear so we're ready for my housewarming party."

"I've got your champagne in my trunk." Harley came to her feet. "And Dyani says Lyndie can't make it because she short staffed at Streams and Meadows. Also, Dyani wants to know if she can bring Fenya Petrova."

"Too bad Lyndie can't make the party." Busy flashed a smile and continued, "Fenya owns the cute wine shop in town, right? Well, you know me, the more the merrier."

Harley didn't tell Busy; Dyani had also asked if she was okay. *Good question. Maybe she'd overreacted to Wyatt not introducing her to Ava as his girlfriend. Maybe if she wanted to keep her handsome sheriff out of the clutches of the brash bitch ... Harley would have to step up her game.*

"Har Har," Busy snapped her fingers, "the cases of champagne aren't going to carry themselves inside."

Harley followed Busy to the Lexus and popped the trunk. They each grabbed a box filled with twelve bottles and carried them up the steps. As she reached the porch, Harley glanced at the house next door, then stepped into Busy's foyer.

"Wyatt Stone belongs to me," she marched to the kitchen and set her box onto the counter, "and I'm not giving him up without a fight."

Busy handed Harley her glass of red wine and clinked their glasses.

"That's my Har Har." Busy lifted her glass, then drained half the contents. "Not that I think Ava Parker has a chance with Wyatt," she smiled at Harley, "but you know how I love a good fight for your man, New York style!"

CHAPTER FOUR

After his mother's piece of shit Ford finally crapped out, Joe began the hunt for a car to steal, settling on a rundown Chevy Malibu. He knew the downside to stealing a readily available car, probably meant the vehicle wasn't in top running condition. But an easy snatch and go had been his best option.

Sticking to back roads, they made good time to Cave Junction and stopped for lunch at an out of the way diner. But when he cranked the engine of the stolen Chevy, it wouldn't engage. He could tell Willow was nervous about him stealing another car. He also wondered if she was curious why after all this time, he was taking her back to Stoneybrook.

"We're going to have to walk through town to find another wreck to steal."

He angled out of the Chevy, rounded the front of the car, and took her hand. Willow glanced at the few belongings she had in the back seat, and he tightened his grip.

"We'll come back for our things." Joe didn't bother to say and clean the car because it was what they'd done with the Ford.

The last time they'd been in Cave Junction, it had been on the way out of Oregon, and he'd kept their exposure to other people to a minimum.

Since Willow spent most of her time chained inside a motel room, she looked like a kid in a candy store as her eyes darted from one shop window to another. Joe wished he could take her shopping in one of the small clothing stores and let her buy a new dress. He admired Willow for trying every day to look nice in her well-worn clothes, but he couldn't risk them being noticed since he'd be stealing a car.

The day was warm, so he popped into a Shop Smart and led Willow to the coolers at the back of the store. He plucked two bottles of water from a shelf, then headed for the checkout.

As they waited behind a man who seemed in a hurry, Willow kept her gaze down as he expected her to do. But when the man abruptly left the checkout line he bumped into her. Startled, Willow looked up. Joe squeezed her hand and Willow's cheeks colored. She glared at him, then looked down again.

"Sorry," the man said as he pushed through the crowd, disappearing toward the back of the store.

The clerk set aside the man's abandoned first aid items. "Find everything you need?" she asked Joe.

"Yes, ma'am." He handed her exactly three dollars and twenty cents to cover the cost of the water and the bottle deposit the state of Oregon charged.

Grabbing the two bottles with one hand, he led Willow from the store. His pulse rate spiked when he saw a flyer showing an age progression photo of Willow Atwood. She didn't notice the picture, so he handed her a water to keep her distracted. Joe stopped on the sidewalk to take a drink from his bottle and Willow opened hers.

There was a Kia Sportage idling at the curb in front of the store. Joe grinned at Willow, then pointed to the other side of the car and stepped to the driver's door.

He climbed behind the wheel and powered off an iPhone connected to a charging station on the dash. Willow buckled her seat belt and he shifted into drive. Joe followed the traffic out of Cave Junction toward the road where they'd left the Malibu.

"We won't have much time." Joe hit the brakes to slow down. The last thing he needed was to be pulled over by a local yocal for speeding in a stolen car. "You grab the stuff from the back seat, and I'll clean out the trunk."

Willow nodded. Once their belongings were in the Kia, he'd proceed to wipe down the surfaces, so they could be on their way.

Switching from one car to the other went smoothly. Joe picked another barely drivable road and headed north. He searched his mental map recalling the terrain around Willow Lake. He tried to dial in on the best place to end his journey with Willow. He knew he should kill her to lessen the possibility of being discovered by law enforcement. But a small thread of humanity buried deep in his soul begged him to let her live.

"I have to pee," Willow said with a quick glance at him.

"Told you not to guzzle your water." Joe chuckled and pulled onto the side of the road. Willow jumped from the car and headed for the tall grass. "Stay where I can see you," he called.

Joe popped the glove box open and pulled out a stack of papers. He thumbed through the wad, stopping on the registration. The name Henry Weber was listed as owner and the section for lien holders was blank.

Joe stepped from the car and stretched. He'd noted the briefcase when he first looked into the car. Surprised the case wasn't locked, he lifted the top to see what was inside. His eyes grew wide at the site of several bundles of one hundred dollar bills. He wanted to take the time to count the money, but he didn't want Willow to know about the cash. He closed the briefcase and lifted the lid of the laptop, which was powered off. Next, he ran his hands along the creases of the car seats and checked the pockets on the back of the front seats. Both searches produced nothing.

Willow had returned and resumed her place in the passenger seat, an earthy scent of wildflowers accompanying her. A whisp of lust snaked through his loins and he contemplated taking her in the back seat of the Kia. But he wanted to treat her to a nice motel room and dinner out, hoping their date night would lead to another pleasant sexual experience. Then he remembered the missing persons poster at the store and reconsidered a night out.

Willow adjusted her seat, and a glint of silver caught his eye. Joe stretched out across the floorboard and reached under the passenger seat. His hand found the gun, but he left it where it was.

Joe settled into the driver's seat and flashed a smile at Willow. Stealing the Kia had been a bright light in their journey. He had money again. If he continued to be frugal, he wouldn't have to find a job right away—or end his time with Willow. The car seemed to be well maintained, so once he switched out the plates, he'd be able to drive the small SUV for a few months. And finding the gun added a layer of security because if he was ever cornered, he'd fight to the death and take Willow with him.

CHAPTER FIVE

Wyatt watched Harley drive away from the Rocky River Bar. He hated that she was crying and wished she had stopped her car. He wanted to wrap her in his arms and apologize.

He scrubbed his face with a hand, then walked back into the bar. Claire and Dyani gave him raised eyebrow stares as he headed to his table.

Ava stood waiting for him; his cowboy hat perched on top of her red hair. A memory of her, naked and wearing his hat as she strutted around the lodge at Willow Lake, flitted through his mind. A thread of desire warmed his loins and he silently cursed himself.

"I boxed up your lunches," Dyani said behind him. "I'm headed for Broken River to help Luke with some mustangs he found tangled in one of the fences, then I'm going to Busy's party."

"Thanks, Dyani." Wyatt gave her a nod. "Have fun at the party."

Dyani shot Ava a look that could melt ice, then walked back to the bar.

Wyatt held out his hand and Ava placed his hat into his open palm. He placed the Stetson on his head and turned to leave.

"Wyatt." Ava grabbed his arm.

"Ava," Wyatt glared at her and pulled his arm free, "I'm going to tell you the same thing I told Blake." He placed his hands on his hips. "I have nothing to say to you."

"I'm sorry." Tears streamed down her cheeks. "I'm truly sorry for hurting you."

Wyatt held his former lover's green eyed stare, nodded, then turned and strode toward the exit. He may have loved Ava at one time, but his feelings for Harley far exceeded whatever he'd felt for Ava. All he could think about was apologizing to Harley for not telling her about Ava and Blake running off together, leaving him devastated at the time. And he hoped it wasn't too late to assure Harley of his love for her.

Once he was outside, he surveyed the damage to his truck, which was minor. Still, it was a county vehicle, so he'd have to arrange to have the damage repaired. He climbed behind the wheel and headed for the station.

After the short drive, Wyatt parked in front of the building and cut the engine. First, Blake was expecting him to listen to whatever lame reason he had for running off with Ava. And now, Ava wanted to explain her part in leaving Stoneybrook with his brother.

He stepped from his truck and walked into the station. Simms and Barnes sat at their desks, eating lunch, the smell of the Babbling Brook Café's Friday chili special permeating the air. Derrick was making notes on a legal pad and Wyatt was relieved not to see Blake.

Wyatt went to the fridge in the kitchenette and placed the boxed lunches inside. He knew he should eat something, but food wasn't his priority. He wanted to wrap up his afternoon and leave for the day. With any luck he could catch Harley at her place before she left for Busy's party.

He'd just sat down when Derrick entered his office, sitting in a chair in front of the desk.

"Wyatt," Derrick looked at him, "Ava's back in town."

Wyatt nodded. "Do you know where Blake went?"

"No." Derrick shook his head and looked past Wyatt out the window behind him. "He got a phone call, looked like he wanted to kill someone, and left." His cousin then looked back at him.

"Anything new on the abandoned and stolen cars?" Wyatt changed the subject.

"Still waiting for reports from Josephine County." Derrick stood. "You should go see Harley." He moved toward the office door. "I can text if we get any actionable information."

Wyatt raised an eyebrow.

"You came back with two TO-GO boxes from lunch." Derrick stared through the open door, then turned and met

Wyatt's gaze. "I'm guessing Ava interrupted your lunch date with Harley and you're worried about her being upset."

Wyatt stood too. "I might stop by the Redneck Ranch on my way to Broken River." He smiled at Derrick. "Keep me posted if you hear anything."

"Copy, Chief." Derrick grinned, then Wyatt followed him as he walked away.

Harley's place was on the way to his ranch, so it wouldn't be inconvenient to see if she was there. As he made the short drive, he contemplated why he hadn't called Harley his girlfriend. They'd dated for over a year and spent most of their free time together. And though they had both said, *I love you*, Wyatt knew his feelings for Harley were stronger than he could verbalize.

He turned into the driveway, noticing Harley's car wasn't parked in the gravel lot behind her house. It was a little early, but Wyatt decided he could start the process of feeding her animals. When he stepped into the barn, Elvis snorted, then flattened his ears and stomped a foot.

"I know big guy," Wyatt stopped in front of the giant horse's stall, "sorry I'm not Harley."

Elvis tossed his head and clomped around his stall. Wyatt made his way through the barn. pygmy goat siblings, Butch and Sundance were munching loose hay and bleated at him in protest as he tried to shoo them away from the alfalfa stack.

"I'll put grain in your bin if you move out of the way." Wyatt pushed on Sundance's rump. After another round of plaintive bleating, the goats bounded out of the barn into the late afternoon sunshine. He tucked an alfalfa straw into the corner of his mouth, the sweet, grassy flavor tickling his tongue. The minis, Rhett and Scarlett rushed their gate when he approached with their hay.

Maverick head butted his stall door and brayed as if someone was pulling on his long ears as Wyatt stepped in front of Trigger's stall.

"You can wait your turn, Maverick." Wyatt noticed Trigger was cowered in a back corner of his stall with his head down. When he saw Wyatt, he tried to bite his side and pawed the ground.

"Hey, Trigger." Wyatt opened the stall door and inched toward the sorrel quarter horse. "You okay, boy?"

Trigger moved toward Wyatt, then tried to bite his flank again, looking like he wanted to drop down and roll. Wyatt knew he couldn't let Trigger lie down and reached for a halter hanging just outside the stall. Once he had the halter secured, Wyatt attached a lead rope and led the horse outside. He thumbed his phone awake and found his foreman's number.

Wyatt: *I think Trigger's in trouble. Colic maybe? Can you come with a trailer?*

As he waited for Luke's reply, Wyatt made a mental note to buy Harley a truck and horse trailer.

Luke: *Working with mustangs. Okay to send Colt?*
Wyatt: *Yes*
Luke: *Copy. I'll let Hannah know about Trigger*

Wyatt secured the horse's rope to the metal fence of the round pen. He vacillated between texting Harley and just taking care of Trigger himself. He didn't want to take her away from Busy's party and ruin her night. But he also knew how much she loved her animals.

Since he'd have about a half hour before Colt arrived with the trailer, Wyatt decided to finish feeding her menagerie, getting them settled for the night. He pulled all the slow feed bags from the other horses' stalls and proceeded to fill them with flakes of hay. He cleaned water buckets and refilled them. Measured out grain for the goats and Hoss, her old hog, then set the portions next to their bins.

When he stepped from the barn, he found Trigger pulling against his rope and trying to kick his belly with a hind hoof. He patted the distressed horse's neck. Harley's mutt, Trampas, sat near Trigger ready to help if needed.

"Let's try some banamine," Wyatt said to Trigger, "maybe a dose and the trailer ride to Broken River will do the trick."

He prepared a syringe with oral paste and walked back to Trigger. The horse's eyes grew wide, but he didn't try to move away from him. He guided the syringe into the back of Trigger's mouth, then pushed the plunger. The horse flattened his ears, then looked at Wyatt with the same *you're not Harley* look Elvis had given him when he first arrived.

Wyatt back tracked into the barn and found a grooming brush. When he returned to Trigger and brushed his flanks, the horse relaxed. He was on his third rotation when Colt arrived with the trailer.

"Hey, Chief," Colt said. "Luke told me to come help you with a sick horse."

"Yes." Wyatt untied the lead rope and led Trigger toward the trailer. "I think this guy has colic. If he doesn't crap on the ride to Broken River, ask the vets to examine him."

"Will do, Chief."

Colt waited until Trigger was secure in the trailer and Wyatt had exited, then he climbed behind the wheel of his truck. He gave Wyatt a wave and drove up Harley's driveway toward Little Creek Road.

Even though it was early, Wyatt decided to finish feeding the other animals. Once he was done, he looked at his phone and debated about what to say in a text to Harley.

Wyatt: *I stopped by your place to see you. Know you're getting ready for Busy's party, so fed your menagerie*

He knew he needed to tell her about Trigger, but wanted to see if she responded first. He hated that she might still be angry with him over their unexpected encounter with Ava. But he was all too familiar with Ms. Harper's temper.

The air had begun to cool as the sun drifted toward the horizon. Honeysuckle rode the breeze blowing to the west. Inhaling the sweet scent, Wyatt wished he could stay and wait for Harley to come home.

Harley: *Crazy here at Busy's. Thanks for feeding my creatures and saving me a trip home*

Wyatt: *Busy's lucky to have you there. Also, Trigger had a raw spot on his abdomen. Had him brought to BR to be checked out*

He didn't like lying to her about Trigger but saw no reason to worry her until the vets examined her horse. He wanted to add, *love you*, but again waited for her reply. He rushed to his truck. As he cranked the engine, his phone buzzed, and he read her text.

Harley: *Is it serious? Should I come to BR?*

Wyatt hesitated because a horse with colic could end badly, but he didn't want to alarm Harley just yet.

Wyatt: *I think he'll be fine. Enjoy the party*

Harley: *Okay. Thanks, Wyatt. Love you*

Wyatt knew he looked like a lovesick fool as he grinned at Harley's text.

Wyatt: *Love you more, Ms. Harper*

CHAPTER SIX

Harley smiled at Wyatt's text and her heart lightened. She wished she could sneak out the back door of Busy's kitchen and race home. The arrival of Ava Parker couldn't be controlled by either of them, but Harley could try to control how the woman affected her relationship with Wyatt.

Despite the urge to be with her handsome sheriff, Harley knew she couldn't abandon Busy. Her bestie was in her element hosting all their Stoneybrook friends in her new home. Plus, by the time she drove to the Redneck Ranch, Wyatt would probably be on his way to Broken River.

"Har Har," Busy called from the living room, "we need more napkins."

Harley grabbed a stack of white napkins embossed with a large, pink B. Even though this party was on a smaller scale than her usual events, Harley knew Busy wanted everything to be perfect.

The doorbell rang as Harley added the napkins to a table sitting at the end of an antique buffet. Busy had turned the top of the vintage cabinet into a charcuterie board. She'd covered the oak surface with foil, then wax paper. Her serpentine of meats, cheeses, and crackers was a masterpiece. She'd also sprinkled nuts, olives, and grapes throughout her design. The tables at each end of the buffet held plates, napkins, and a small platter of chocolates.

Busy opened the door and found Claire Norman and Mercy Edwards standing on her porch. Claire held a bag of dripping ice and Mercy juggled a vase of flowers with a container of cookies.

"Come in," Busy took the bag of ice, "I'll put this in the freezer."

Harley took the vase of multi-colored dahlia's and placed them in the center of the fireplace mantel.

"Where should I put the cookies?" Mercy asked.

"Next to the chocolates on the dessert table at the end of the buffet." Harley pointed.

"Harley," Claire grasped her hands, "I'm so sorry Ava ruined your lunch with Wyatt."

"It's okay, Claire." Harley smiled.

"No, it's not," Claire shook her head, "that bitch is like a bad penny, always showing up at the wrong time."

"And she has the morals of an alley cat." Mercy frowned. "I believe it's her goal to torture poor Wyatt for as long as she can."

"Wyatt and I are fine." Harley smiled. "It should be me apologizing for storming off."

"If you want my opinion," Busy joined them, "Miss Parker has no idea what's in store for her from a couple of New Yawkers." She smiled at Harley. "We know how to deal with a brassy, redheaded bitch."

They laughed and Harley knew Busy would make sure Ava Parker paid for hurting her bestie. Harley's main concern though, was keeping hers and Wyatt's relationship on track.

The bell rang again, and the door swung open to reveal Hannah Sloan and Ella Night.

"Welcome!" Busy hugged them. "You two look fabulous."

"Thanks, Busy." Hannah brushed a strand of strawberry blonde hair from her face. "It was a rush job, but we're here."

"Everything okay?" Harley asked.

Ella nodded. "Luke brought in a colt and four mustangs. The colt was attacked by something. Plus, the adult horses have cuts from barbwire fencing, so we've been busy treating them."

"And we got Trigger settled into an exam room," Hannah added, "so far no manure, but Luke's watching him."

"Trigger's in good hands, Har Har," Busy handed Hannah and Ella flutes of champagne, "so, let's get this party started."

The word manure floated through Harley's mind. *Hadn't Wyatt said Trigger had a raw spot? If so, then why were the vets concerned about her horse not pooping?*

Before she could ask questions, Busy handed her a flute of champagne.

"Welcome to Stoneybrook, Busy." Claire held her glass aloft.

"You are such a breath of fresh air, and we're glad you finally moved here." Mercy clinked Claire's glass.

A round of pings followed as they touched each other's glasses, then took sips of champagne. A double knuckle rap was followed by Dyani opening the door and stepping inside.

"Hey." She gave a slight wave. "You all remember Fenya?"

"Of course. I love your wine shop, Fenya," Busy said, "and what a clever name, A STONE'S THROW."

"Thank you." The Russian beauty's cheeks colored.

"Let's get you ladies a glass of bubbly." Busy headed for the bar she had installed before moving in.

Harley had toured the quaint two story Victorian with Busy, who she could tell had fallen in love with the charming house. Busy had decided the front room, which had a large picture window, would be the perfect entertainment space. All it needed, her bestie had declared, was an antique bar to complete the room. Busy had placed the bar in a corner on one side of a red brick fireplace and the buffet occupied the other corner. A couch and two overstuffed armed chairs completed the space.

"Harley," Claire said, Mercy looking over her shoulder. "Is Ria still coming with Sylvie?"

"Yes." Harley nodded. "And I believe Ria talked Echo into coming too."

"She did," Mercy stepped in front of Claire, "Echo is coming with Mia and Marie Davis. They're bringing Busy's gift."

"That's great!" Harley clapped her hands together.

"What's great?" Busy asked as she joined them.

"Ria," Harley began, "um, she finally convinced Echo to come tonight too."

"I'm so glad." Busy smiled. "And is Sylvie coming?"

"Yes." Claire nodded. "Ria said her assistant is ready to put her kidnapping ordeal behind her."

"Fantastic!" Busy said. "Har Har, can you help me in the kitchen?"

"Sure." As Harley followed Busy, her phone chimed.

"Wyatt?" Busy walked into the kitchen.

Harley looked at her phone and nodded.

Wyatt: *Trigger's sore isn't worrisome*

"Go ahead and text with your handsome sheriff," Busy said, pulling a tray of puff pastries with brie and mushrooms from the oven. A buttery aroma filled the air as she placed the tiny hors d'oeuvres onto a platter.

"Thanks, Busy," Harley began her text, "I'll bring the crab cakes."

Harley: *Thanks for the update, but why are the vets worried about Trigger pooping? You're sure he's doing okay?*

Wyatt: *I'll explain when I see you, but yes, he's doing better. How's the party?*

Harley: *Alright. Party's good*

Wyatt: *Still on for dinner at your place tomorrow?*

Harley: *Yes. Can't wait!*

When he didn't text right back, Harley took the crab cakes from the second oven. She was tempted to carry the cookie sheet back to the living room. Instead, she used a spatula to set the cakes onto a round amber-colored plate.

Wyatt hadn't texted again, so Harley headed back to the party. As she entered the front room, the door swung open and Mayor, Ria Stone, stepped inside. Sylvie Owen followed, and Harley noticed her previous haughty demeanor still seemed subdued. A shudder traveled down her spine with the memory of what Sylvie Owen had suffered at the hands of Carl Yates. Harley understood and admired the young woman's determination to move on with her life.

"Ria," Busy said, "I'm glad you and Sylvie could come."

"We're honored to be included," Ria said and handed Busy a wine bag imprinted with A STONE'S THROW. "I hope this helps you feel welcomed to Stoneybrook." She looked at Sylvie.

"Yes." Sylvie handed Busy another bag. "Welcome to Stoneybrook."

"I thought I was clear in my invitation that the only gift I wanted was your presence." Busy smiled. "But then again, what girl doesn't love presents!"

"Please, ladies," Harley said, "grab a plate and enjoy Busy's delicious appetizers."

Busy moved closer to Harley and whispered, "My new life here wouldn't be as fabulous without you and all your friends."

"They're your friends now too." Harley picked up a flute from the bar and touched Busy's glass. "And if I haven't told you already, I'm so glad you moved to Stoneybrook."

"Me too—" A knock caused Busy to look toward the door, then at Harley as everyone gathered around her. "Harley Harper," Busy raised an eyebrow, "what did you do?"

Harley smiled at her bestie as the door opened revealing a large welcome sign painted on an old piece of barn wood. The word welcome was stenciled in black and below the last *E*, the words, New Yawk, had been painted in cursive. Mia and Marie, along with Echo Atwood, stood behind the sign.

Tears filled Busy's eyes, and she'd covered her mouth with her hands, then glanced around the room.

"We're all glad you moved here." Claire raised her glass.

"To Elizabeth Benton!" Harley held her glass in the air. "Stoneybrook's second favorite New Yorker."

A round of laughter filled the living room as Harley's phone chimed.

Wyatt: *I think you should come to BR*

Harley raised her eyes to find Ella looking at her and Hannah checking her phone. Her vets walked toward Busy who glanced at Harley.

"Sorry, Busy," Hannah said, "but we need to get back to Broken River." She stepped to Mia and Marie and gave them each a hug. "Mom, Luke and I might miss family dinner on Sunday, I'll keep you posted."

"Hannah," Busy said, "take Harley with you." She crossed to Harley and wrapped her in a hug. "Trigger will be all right, but you should be with him."

Harley nodded, then followed Hannah and Ella outside. She climbed into the backseat of Hannah's truck and thumbed her phone alive.

Harley: *I'm riding to BR with the vets*

Wyatt: *Glad you're coming. We're doing everything we can*

Tears slipped down Harley's cheeks. Staring out the window at the waning light, she silently apologized for not being a better horse mom. She promised to improve her animal skills if her sorrel quarter horse recovered. Finally, she said a prayer asking God to heal Trigger.

**"WILLOW'S WOODS" WILL BE AVAILABLE
SUMMER 2024**